The Abduction of Lilly Waters

By
T.M. Novak

Court Jester Publications

Naugatuck, CT\

The Abduction of Lilly Waters

This book is dedicated to:

To my children, Wyatt, Gage, Cole and Cru, who've been by my side through all the goals I've set my mind to. You support me endlessly and never complain about the hours I spend in front of the computer screen. I love you all.

To my family, who showed their support any way they could. My brothers and sisters are a huge part of who I am. I love them and the ones who became a part of them. Family is truly a blessing. You're all loved very much and I thank you for your support.

To my friends and people who love me, you know who you are!

To my sister Latisha Wood, who put time and energy into drawing a custom cover. It is truly amazing. Thank you. I love you forever.

Chapter 1

Thank God the diner was still open, she thought as she turned off the car engine. She had to pee like never before. The rain was pouring down in thick, unforgiving sheets, pounding against the rusted metal of her car. She turned around in her seat to check on her sleeping daughter. The sight warmed her chilled body. At first, she considered letting Lilly stay in the car, but she dismissed it before it could find a reasonable place in her thoughts. Beth absolutely hated the idea of waking her daughter from her peaceful slumber, but she knew leaving her wasn't an option. What if Lilly woke up while she was gone? She felt defeated by the situation. Beth turned back, grabbing her long overcoat off the seat next to her. It was a struggle to put it on while still seated in the driver's seat, but she wanted to be ready to cover Lilly with it. Satisfied she had everything she needed to make a quick exit, she braced herself for the rain and reached for the door handle.

"This is it, the moment of truth," she huffed as she grabbed her keys. The idea of getting soaked wasn't pleasing. It was just her luck not to be prepared for a rainstorm on a road trip in the middle of tornado alley. She opened the car door and stepped into the torrential rain that wasted no time pelting her with its stinging drops.

Even her unborn baby protested, giving her gut a hard kick. Beth thought her bladder would let go right then and there from the jolt. With great haste, she opened the back door, exposing her sleeping daughter to the elements.

"Sweetheart, you have to wake up. Mommy has to go potty again," Beth whispered as she gently stroked her daughter's soft cheek.

The diner's lights flickered as they struggled to stay on through the pouring rain and lightning that streaked across the stormy sky. Thick streams of rain poured inside the car as Beth wrestled to unlatch the car seat.

Lilly was a good-natured girl, and she didn't protest the intrusion; instead, she threw her arms around her mother's neck while she was clumsily plucked from the car. The teddy bear Lilly was holding tumbled from her hands, landing on the floorboard.

Beth struggled to place her coat over her daughter's head, but the rain was so heavy it wasn't much help. She felt horrible as water splattered onto Lilly's face. She pulled her daughter closer to her

2

body. Lilly was small for her age, but her weight wasn't easy to bear with Beth's pregnant tummy and protesting bladder.

"Sweetie, you'll have to walk once we get inside, and walk fast because Mommy has to pee really, really bad. Okay, baby?"

Beth took quick, cautious steps toward the entrance of the diner. She didn't want to fall with Lilly in her arms.

Inside the warm, dry restaurant, Beth instantly spotted the neon bathroom sign hanging on the back wall. It seemed like a distant oasis beckoning her. Carefully, she set Lilly down, making sure she was awake enough to walk without trouble. Grabbing Lilly's hand, she scurried across the floor, practically dragging her sleepy daughter along with her. Oh God, she didn't think she'd make it. A feeling of annoyance filled her, causing her blood to boil. *Who the hell puts wash rooms in the back of a restaurant?* she wondered angrily, although before this moment, she'd never cared where they were.

There were only a few people scattered through the quiet place, but they didn't pay her any mind. She was relieved, because she didn't feel like putting on a friendly face.

Once they finally reached the bathroom, she shoved the door open, thrilled it was unoccupied. It was tiny and smelled of overused lemon Lysol. There was only one stall, and she lunged for it. She tugged Lilly forward, trying to fit the two of them in the small enclosure. Her pregnant belly squished poor Lilly against the wall and once they were both in, Beth couldn't close the door.

"Dammit," she cursed through gritted teeth.

"Lilly, honey, we don't both fit in the stall. You're going to have to wait outside the door while Mommy goes potty, okay?"

With great reluctance, she placed Lilly right where she wanted her to stand and let go of her hand. "Now you stand right here and sing Mommy a song. Keep your feet right under the door where I can see them," she added in a quiet whisper as she gazed into her daughter's brown eyes.

Lilly didn't speak, she simply nodded and with hesitation, Beth shut the stall door. Her daughter's feet were right where she asked Lilly to place them.

"Lilly, can you sing Mommy a song?" she called through the door to her daughter.

4

Beth hated the idea of leaving her little girl outside the stall. She loathed doing anything that might create fear for her. Comfort washed over Beth as she heard her daughter sing "Twinkle, Twinkle Little Star" in her tiny, soft voice. She could still see Lilly's shiny, red leather shoes right where she'd asked her to place them, except now they were tapping to the beat of the song.

Lilly's sweet voice was also a sad reminder to Beth that "Twinkle, Twinkle, Little Star" was the only children's song she knew, and in turn, it was the only song Lilly had to choose from. Sometimes Beth would catch Lilly singing a made-up song and thought it was so adorable how her little girl could make them up right on the spot. Singing was one of Lilly's favorite things to do to pass the time.

Beth could hear Lilly from the back seat of the car most of the trip singing and humming to herself in such contentment that it warmed Beth's heart. Leaving town wasn't the easiest choice she'd made, but it was a necessary choice in order to start a fresh life and escape her horrific past.

As she watched Lilly's dancing feet, she knew she had to make a point to learn more songs to teach her. Beth couldn't help but smile at the possibilities her new life would hold. Her daughter gave her faith. Lilly's voice bounced off the bathroom walls in all directions. The calming sound made Beth's mind wander to the new baby inside her. The new baby would bring her great happiness, too. It's amazing the hope a baby growing inside you can bring. Anything seemed possible.

Distracted by her thoughts, Beth hadn't noticed that Lilly had already completed the song. She was about to ask Lilly to start the song again when she noticed Lilly's feet move ever so slightly.

"Lilly, make sure you stay right there. Mommy is almost done."

The last thing Beth wanted was for Lilly to walk out of the bathroom alone. Good God, the thought frightened her. In that instant, she thought she heard a small tap on the other side of the bathroom. Lilly was still where she'd left her because she could see her daughter's tiny red shoes.

"Lilly? You gonna sing a song again for Mommy?"

The silence that followed was eerie. Was someone in the bathroom now? That's the only thing Beth could think of.

"Is someone there?" She paused a moment, but didn't hear a response. "Lilly baby, is someone out there with you?" Lilly didn't answer. Her daughter's feet were slightly turned in the direction of the bathroom door. Then, in one quick motion, Lilly's feet disappeared from sight. Beth's heart leaped into her throat.

Beth knew Lilly couldn't have jumped. She was only three and still unable to jump fully off the ground. Terror filled her soul. Anger and fear rushed through her. She flew to her feet, pulling up her clothes.

"Who's there? You put my daughter back! You're going to scare her!" A startling silence followed. The kind of hush you don't want to hear when a child is around, or supposed to be around.

Beth fumbled for the stall door. The terror of the moment gripped her stomach. Her fingers wouldn't work, and tears pooled in her eyes. Something in her soul shouted a warning, but the lock refused to work. Panic crashed in around her.

Screaming was the only form of defense she had left. She yelled as she pounded on the stall door.

But her daughter's voice didn't reply. Sucking in her fear, she tried once again to unlock the stubborn bathroom lock. Finally, she was able to get it to click, and she threw the door open. It slammed with a loud bang against the side wall. She didn't know how much time had passed. It must've only been several seconds, but seconds when a child's safety is concerned is too long. The bathroom was empty; Lilly was gone.

Chapter 2

Beth flew from the bathroom, searching the restaurant. Her eyes darted from side to side, high and low, penetrating the room feverishly. The dining area was dimly lit, making it difficult to see all corners of the room.

"Lilly, Lilly, where are you?" she shouted. Lilly was nowhere in sight. "Somebody, help me!" she choked as she raced back and forth, afraid to move too far from the bathroom.

A man sitting at the counter near the center of the diner folded his newspaper slowly and turned to gaze in her direction. He turned his attention back to someone just out of Beth's view and she watched as he chuckled and rolled his eyes.

Beth knew she had to make the seriousness of the situation known because time was ticking by. She knew she must look crazy, so she tried to calm herself before she spoke again. "My little girl was just taken from the bathroom."

The man and woman sitting at the table closest to Beth turned and gaped at her with open mouths. Beth lunged at them, baffled by their blank stares. She slapped her hand down in front of

9

them, wishing she could pound some concern into them. Coffee toppled from the gentleman's cup. His face grew irritated as he questioned Beth's motive with his eyes. He slowly stood, waving his hands. "Ma'am, we ain't seen no little girl."

Beth looked at him oddly. *How could they not have seen her?* she thought to herself, bewildered by the idea. She pleaded with her eyes for him to say something more, but he simply tilted his head dumbly, returning his attention back to his female friend as he sat back down.

A fire sweltered under Beth's skin. She wanted nothing more than to slap the bushy, overgrown beard right off his face. She was about to do just that when a redheaded waitress approached her from behind.

"Now Ma'am, just calm down. There is no reason to shout." The waitress held her hand up in a calming motion.

Beth slapped her hand away and turned to the front door. There was no way whoever took Lilly could have gotten far, or escaped unseen. She proceeded past the couple's table, pushing aside the annoying waitress, who obviously knew nothing. She checked under tables as she moved along, holding her swollen belly with one hand while lifting checkered tablecloths with the other. She moved along quickly, looking under each table she reached. Once the waitress caught up to Beth, she grabbed her by the arm, stopping her from moving any further.

The redheaded waitress towered over Beth, who was barely five feet tall; it didn't take much to hold her tiny frame still. Beth could see concern growing on the lady's face as her thickly painted eyes squinted together, assessing the situation.

"Ma'am, you need to calm down," the waitress said in her thick Okie accent. Her blue eyes grew smaller as she struggled to get Beth to face her. Her thin, bony fingers gripped Beth's arms firmly, giving her no possibility of pulling away. With pleading words, the waitress was able to get Beth to stop and focus on her. "You need to calm down and explain to me what's wrong. I can't help you if I don't know what's going on."

Beth's eyes spilled over with tears. She didn't know what had happened. How was she supposed to explain it to someone else? She felt so confused. All she knew was her little girl wasn't where she'd left her. Through sloppy words, she told the waitress what had happened. Fear gripped her again as she told the story. She had to find Lilly. Beth twisted her hands free and ran towards the entrance of the restaurant, determined to continue her search. She wanted to check the parking lot. There was no time to lose. As she ran out the front door, she heard the waitress yell, "I think we need to call the cops. That lady just said her daughter was taken."

Chapter 3

Outside in the ominous night, the rain slapped Beth across the face.

"Lilly!" Her scream pierced the darkness, meeting the relentless thunder as it cracked against the black sky. It was like a battle of wills, each trying to conquer the other. *This can't be happening,* she thought as she pressed her face to the glass of her car, hoping with every fiber in her she'd find her daughter asleep in the back seat. Nothing was there.

Terror gripped Beth from the depth of her being, and her mind escaped her body altogether, floating above her head like a leaf tossed in the wind. Beth slapped her cheeks. She knew if she didn't get control of her emotions, she'd never recover her daughter again. She refused her legs the right to crumble from under her, even though her body begged to fall. Now wasn't the time to allow weakness. She turned her attention to the other cars in the parking lot. Beth ran through the rain and searched each vehicle she saw, and each time she found nothing, her heart threatened to break.

It felt like her world was tumbling out of control. She wanted to stop it, but she couldn't. Her head was dizzy. The thunder and lightning of reality smashed down on her. Beth spun around, searching for more cars to check, but there weren't any. She didn't know how long she'd wandered through the parking lot because time had stopped. It felt like she was lost in a wind tunnel swirling around and around. As her legs finally collapsed from under her, she felt a hand grip her shoulder.

Beth turned, expecting to see the maniac who took Lilly. She silently hoped the person realized their mistake and returned her, but when she looked up, she saw a man holding a police badge in his hand. The officer waved his badge in her face and his lips mouthed words she couldn't hear.

Beth gazed past him, desperate to discover something she'd missed. Her weak voice pleaded out loud for this to not be happening to her. "I have to find her!" stammered Beth. "I have to find my daughter." Her bottom lip quivered and the police officer gripped her tighter. This time, he held her by the shoulders with two strong hands. Beth was grateful for that. His hands grounded her to reality, even if the reality was one she didn't want to face.

His brown eyes searched her face; concern etched into every crease on his face. Abruptly, the spinning slowed and she could hear his words.

"We will find your little girl, but we need to know what happened here. I am Detective Daniel Prescott. Please try to calm down. Focus on your breathing." His hands held firm to Beth's shoulders and his gentle eyes pleaded for her to focus.

Beth caught her breath and locked her eyes on the officer. In her heart, she knew this man would help her, so she let her story spill forth.

"Lilly, Lilly is gone." Her lips trembled. Grief filled her voice. She sucked back the sobs that wanted to escape and flew forward with as many details as she could. It was exhausting and Beth was worried she'd overlooked something, but it had all been so confusing, and it happened so fast.

The police officer leaned in close and took Beth under the arm. He led her gently under the awning and out of the worst of the rain. The thunder and lightning crashed around them, drowning out her voice with each jolt.

"Focus on my face, stay with me, and just think back. Tell me everything you can remember."

She gazed intently into his eyes. They gave her strength to go on.

It wasn't long before a second officer joined them. She noticed he wasn't dressed in a uniform, either. The only way Beth knew he was a cop was by the badge encased in leather that dangled from a chain around his neck.

"This is my partner, Frank Martinez."

The concern on his face mirrored the look on Detective Prescott's face. It was then Beth realized there were blue and red lights flashing everywhere. The parking lot was alive with activity. It was as if the bubble that enclosed her had instantly burst. The reality of life exploded around her.

It was a certainty she didn't want to face. There was a startling flash of lightning and Beth's attention turned to her car. There was a detail coming back to her she'd ignored earlier because when she first looked in the car, she wasn't looking for details. Instead, she was looking for her daughter.

The detective noticed the switch in Beth's focus, and his intent look followed hers. Beth managed to stumble towards her car. Her feet slapped the soggy pavement in loud smacks. The cold water splashed up her legs in dirty splatters.

Detective Prescott caught up and grabbed her arm once again. "What is it?" he asked.

Beth stopped, and her free hand crept to her throat. She pulled away and raced across the pavement. With an unsteady hand, she dug through her skirt pocket and found her keys. She needed to see inside the car. Beth struggled with the car handle and swung the door open. What she found would haunt her forever. It would replay in her mind over and over, reminding her continuously that she was never in control. Her fate had been sealed before she stepped one foot into the restaurant. The two detectives followed her to the car. Beth couldn't believe her eyes. Her stomach heaved as she forced the bile back down. Leaning into the car, she moved things around, as if it would do any good. Lilly's car seat was gone and so we all of her belongings, including the stuffed bear Lilly had been sleeping with when they arrived at the diner.

Detective Prescott peered over her shoulder and Beth could hear him asking, "What is it?"

Beth's world crashed in around her as the reality of the moment snuffed her mind into darkness.

Chapter 4

Detective Prescott lifted the lady's limp body from the ground where she'd fallen moments before. She was a small woman, and even with her swollen belly, she couldn't have been much more than a hundred and twenty pounds. It took little effort to carry her to the waiting paramedics, who were pulling up. He wanted to get answers from her, but he knew it could be a while before she'd be able to speak coherently. As he glanced around, he realized he had nothing to go on. The rain had lessened, and he wished it was an indication of good things to come. The woman was a complete mess when he had first approached her, but he knew something in the car had sent her mind into darkness. It was that split second that caused the greatest curiosity.

He'd been in this position before. Missing children were never the ideal assignment. He always found it difficult to be compassionate and yet keep the distance required to do the job. It was an emotionally and mentally arduous task to sift through their ever-evolving stories, all the while trying to stay focused on the job at hand, which was getting the kid back safe and sound. And then there were the cases where the parents were the perpetrators. He'd never understand why or how parents could harm their own children. Praying this woman wasn't one of them, his eyes scanned across the bustling parking lot. Watching the scene unfold brought him back to where his darkest memory lay hidden. He thought back to his past missing children's cases. The one that disturbed him the most was when a mother claimed to be carjacked. The thief in question supposedly took her car with her two children still strapped in the back. She had so many realistic details, and her story seemed plausible.

The car was later found at the bottom of a steep cliff. The two boys were both dead. The entire South Carolina police force was determined to find the evil person who'd done this to the children.

Daniel was young and naïve then, just starting his police career. He'd believed the mother's story like most of America, but there were many people who didn't believe her. They said her lies were evident on film, and they were right. In the end, it turned out the mother pushed her own car off the cliff, killing her children. He was completely bewildered when the story unraveled and the truth emerged. The woman in the case was selfishly insane to commit such a crime, and her reasoning left the world dumbfounded. Sane people couldn't understand her reasoning.

She was about to enter a divorce and thought getting rid of her children would save her marriage. The woman claimed her husband felt trapped by fatherhood. Daniel was horrified by the story. How could she have done such a thing? As he looked back now with a well-trained eye, he could see all the telltale signs that she was a liar. Back then, though, he'd missed all of them. It was missing those signs then that caused his lack of confidence today.

That event was a turning point in his life. It was why he decided he wanted to be a detective. He transferred to Moore, Oklahoma, shortly after that famous case. Staying in that town was too painful. The cliff was a constant reminder of how cruel and selfish people could be and how no one could ever fully be trusted.

The fact that the mom was guilty wasn't the only defining moment for him. Daniel would forever be haunted by the image of the car being hoisted back up. He stood by the side of the road when they tried to pry the mangled car door open. In the back passenger side window, he could see a tiny hand resting lifeless against the window. The poor children had no chance. There were still times

Daniel woke up sweating and crying out with that image playing over and over in his nightmare. Detective Prescott hoped this time the ending would be a happy one. Time was critical. He had to work fast.

As the paramedics took the woman from his arms, Daniel stepped back to talk with his partner. The rain finally lightened to a sporadic mist, but it didn't affect the heavy burden that weighed on his shoulders or his mind. He crossed his arms over his chest.

"I'm going to ride with her to the hospital. If I can get a jump on her story, it will help us out," stated Daniel.

Detective Martinez grunted his approval. They'd both been through this before. Too many deaths, too much heartache. Each time, it felt the same, regardless of the conditions. Always the nagging questions, like what could they have done differently? Did they miss something important? Did they follow the wrong lead? In the end, somehow, they found a way to move on. The next case was waiting, but lately the pain was just too heavy to carry.

They needed to feel success, and the sensation of a warm child in their arms. They wanted to feel like there was still something worth fighting for. They wanted to feel like they could still make a difference.

Martinez was obviously still feeling pessimistic as a result of their last case. His teeth were grinding together and his lips pursed as he turned to Daniel. "You wake up that woman, and let's get this started. I want to get to the bottom of this, and now." He stepped closer to Daniel. "I'll hang back here for a bit and go through the restaurant and parking lot with a fine-tooth comb." He paused briefly as he pulled a pack of smokes from his breast pocket. "When I think I've seen and heard all there is to see, I'll join you at the hospital." He gave the pack a hard tap, causing one to fall from the square opening. Fingers trembling with caffeine energy, plucked the cigarette from the box. "I'll get a team together to do a double check after I leave. Don't let her out of your sight. Don't let a single question go unanswered." He pointed the cigarette in Daniel's face while he barked orders. "You find out what she was doing here in the middle of the night with a little girl and a pregnant belly. I want to know everything." Frank placed the cigarette in his mouth. He pulled out a lighter, lit his cigarette, sucking in a long drag of smoke.

Martinez only smoked when he was worried about something, and given the situation, Daniel couldn't blame him. "Find out what startled her in the car. And I don't know if you've noticed, but there is a broken window on the passenger side," he pointed briskly in the direction of the car, which was already being searched by police. "It looks like someone broke in," he added. "What doesn't make sense is, if the girl was with the mother, then why is there a broken window on the car? Not to mention, her purse is still on the floor of the front seat." He scratched his head.

Something isn't right here, Daniel thought as he turned his stare back up to his partner. The ideas were swirling around in his brain. He was trying really hard to figure the case out, but there was so much left to discover, and he was approaching this case with no sleep. While Frank was home cozying up to his wife, Daniel had yet to leave the station. Considering all Frank had suggested, Daniel tried to shake off his fatigue, but the gesture didn't go unnoticed. He could feel Frank eyeing him; sympathy oozed from his concerned stare.

"Daniel, Jen said you just left the station when the call came in. She said you were still sifting through the files of the Jones case.

24

I told her to file them for us. You don't need that case keeping you up anymore." He eyeballed his partner, driving his point home with a troubled glance.

Daniel didn't answer Martinez's last plea; he simply nodded in agreement, knowing full well his partner was right.

"Get some answers!" was Frank's final order before he walked toward the diner.

Daniel knew Martinez was fired up. He'd seen him like this before. On their last investigation, Martinez felt strongly the parents were involved, but Daniel pulled him in another direction. He should have listened to his partner. The outcome would've been much better if he had. He couldn't blame Martinez for approaching this one with such anger. This time, he must not let his emotions get in the way. He decided it was best if Martinez stayed back and sorted through the scene. His partner was too fired up, and the risk was high, he'd say the wrong thing. Daniel knew the lady trusted him. It was visible in her eyes.

Daniel was glad Martinez was so on fire right now, because it rejuvenated him. It made him feel like maybe this time it would be different.

"Oh, and find out about the baby daddy," Martinez yelled to Daniel as he pulled the diner door open. "I want to know where he is."

Daniel waved him off and jumped into the waiting ambulance. His body shivered as his adrenalin slowed. It was going to be a very long night.

Chapter 5

In the ambulance, the incoherent mother was being examined for any obvious signs of injury, but there were none. Daniel was concerned, but he knew he needed to start asking questions immediately. The EMT was administering an IV and taking initial vitals while sirens wailed above them as they headed toward the hospital.

He eyed the EMT nervously. "How is she?"

The young woman looked at Daniel, and annoyance filled her eyes. He could tell she didn't like having police officers hovering over her. She turned away from his stare. "She is weak, but she appears stable. I'm going to give her something to relax her for now. She seems to be having mild contractions, and we don't know how far along she is in the pregnancy. We can't have her going into labor until we know more." She grabbed a syringe from a drawer and prepared it for an injection. Tiny droplets of the fluid dripped from the tip of the needle.

Daniel grabbed her hand, holding tight. "You can't."

The EMT looked at him, anger obvious in her eyes.

"I can, and I am! Just who do you think you are?" Her dark eyes were cold as stone. "We need to make sure she doesn't go into labor. If you don't like it, then you can get out of my rig and walk to the hospital."

He caught her stare and the message it held. It wasn't a threat but a promise, and Daniel knew she was serious, but she had no idea how serious he was, too. He wasn't going to let her win the battle of wills that was raging between them, but he decided it was best to change his approach.

He smiled slowly, letting his charm fill his features. "Ma'am, I realize you're concerned about your patient. I am too, but I'm also concerned about a missing little girl and if you take that needle and stick her, we won't have the answers we need in order to find this woman's child for Lord knows how long."

He didn't let go of the EMT's wrist. He could tell his words hadn't yet hit home. She was still viewing him as an enemy.

"Look here, officer?"

"Detective…." he cut her off.

"Detective," she spat. "If she goes into labor and the baby in there isn't ready, then there will be hell to pay. It's my job to protect her health and the child's health, so let go of my arm," she demanded through gritted teeth.

Daniel could feel her pull away, and his grip tightened. He leaned closer so she could see the determination in his eyes before he spoke again. "I understand that, and I commend you for your commitment, but the baby right there is snug and cozy inside its Mama, and no harm is immediate." He paused to emphasize the passion his next words held. "What about the little girl that is missing? Does she get denied the right for someone to fight for her safety? The answers I need are being held by that woman. Every minute that ticks by makes it harder to find the child that is missing, out in this cold, with Lord knows who, getting Lord knows what done to her." He emphasized the word 'Lord,' making it long and drawn out. "Now, you have the choice to save one child, or two." He paused, locking his eyes on his opponent, hoping his words pierced her stubborn barrier. "What's it gonna be?"

He didn't have to wait for an answer. The tension in her shoulders slowly evaporated. He could see she wasn't a completely heartless woman.

She didn't speak immediately, but finally let out a sigh. "I can give her something that will wake her up. It won't hurt the baby. You can ask her whatever you need." She paused. "I pray you find the poor little girl."

Daniel slowly released her wrist. "You and me both," he replied with an exhausted sigh. He sat back, waiting patiently as he watched for signs of consciousness from the young mother. Her eyes twitched for several seconds and slowly fluttered opened.

Recognition flashed as she opened her glassy eyes, and tears escaped from the corners. Daniel leaned forward and tried to comfort the pregnant lady. He could imagine she must be reliving the last hour. It had to be painful. Her cries picked up conviction, and before long, she was wailing. He instinctively laid his hand on her forehead and brushed back her damp curls. "Shhhh, Ma'am, we're going to help you. I need to ask you some questions." He paused to let his words find their target.

Her eyes darted around the rig. With great determination, she wiped the tears from her face. Her pale skin was blotched with grief and her eyes were dark and pained. He tried to ignore the vulnerability she represented. He couldn't let his guard down. At least that's what he kept telling himself.

"We met at the diner. I'm Detective Daniel Prescott of the Moore police department." He paused, not wanting to get too formal with her. He knew if he acted like a friend, he'd have a better chance of keeping her confidence. "You can call me Daniel."

She eyed him cautiously, giving him her attention the best she could.

"What's your name?" He had to start with the most basic question.

Her voice cracked as she slowly released the words. "Beth. Beth Waters," she replied.

"Beth Waters," he repeated as he pulled out his notebook.

"Beth, I need to know your little girl's name, and what she was wearing and anything you can tell me so we can put out an Amber alert right way. Concern etched his face after he spoke. He paused briefly as he watched her try to control her trembling. "Can you do that for me?"

Beth's lip quivered. Her face twisted in sorrow. "Yes. I can. Her name is Lilly. She is three years old. She was wearing this cute little jumper dress. It's pink with tiny little ladybugs on it." The details flew forth with animation as her hands relayed the story along with her words. "She was wearing a turtleneck top under the jumper and it had lady bugs, too." Beth stopped to catch her breath. Tears filled her eyes once again.

Daniel stopped writing and closed his notebook. He shoved it carelessly back into his breast pocket. Deep sadness filled his thoughts. His brown eyes found her troubled stare, and he wished he could tell her it was all a horrible dream. He couldn't, though.

"It's okay to be worried. I'm worried too, but we're going to do what we can to find her." He stopped briefly before he continued. "Do you happen to have a photograph of her anywhere?"

"We stopped at a carnival earlier and I had a portrait done of her. It's in my car."

"Where in your car?" He could tell she was trying to remember, so he waited patiently for the reply.

"I was buckling Lilly in the car, and I think I placed it in the seatback pocket. I don't remember for sure. I could've put it in Lilly's suitcase. If I did, then it's gone. Her suit case wasn't in the car when I looked in it."

Concern grew on the detective's face. His brows furrowed as his anxiety hit its peak. "What do you mean, gone?"

"When I looked in the car, before I passed out, I noticed Lilly's suitcase, car seat, and teddy bear were missing. Someone took them!"

He scratched the tip of his nose. He knew something startled Beth back at the parking lot, but this information added a new dimension to the case. He had never heard of a kidnapping case where the perp took time to take a car seat and suitcase, let alone a teddy bear. Kidnappers were in too much of a hurry to bother with belongings. Instantly, he doubted his victim. Stubbornly, he folded his arms across his chest and slumped back in his seat while heaving a heavy sigh. Slowly, his gaze turned upwards as he stared blankly at the ceiling of the ambulance. He waited there momentarily as he thought to himself. Finally, he sat back up and faced her.

"Okay, I need to contact my team and let them know what I know so far. I want to have them look for that sketch, and check the car for prints. If someone went in your car to take those things, then they could've left some kind of evidence behind." He tried hard to

33

make his words sound convincing. Internally, he was worried as hell. He didn't mention he knew about a broken window.

Sometimes parents of missing kids slip up and reveal information they shouldn't know, and Beth shouldn't know about the broken window. Daniel needed her to slip up and mention it. He pulled out his cell phone and placed the call.

"Hey, Frank. It's me." Daniel relayed the information. "Listen, there is supposed to be a sketch of the little girl in the pocket of the car behind the seat. Can you look for it?"

Beth could hear a faint voice on the other end of the phone. She couldn't make out any words, but she silently prayed he'd find the drawing. It took several moments for the voice to return to the phone.

"Yeah. That's it. Great. Get an Amber alert out right away. That sketch is the most current image of the little girl. Do a complete workup on the car. I'll call you back in a few minutes," Daniel said hastily. He hung up and smiled at Beth, trying to bring her some comfort.

"It was right where you said it would be." He grinned broadly at Beth.

The ambulance pulled into the emergency room entrance. He knew he would soon have doctors pushing him aside, and he needed to know more, so he asked the EMT to help him stall for a few minutes more.

She went to the driver and spoke in a hushed whisper. The rig stopped, and the driver got out, asking the doctors to wait a few more minutes. Daniel could hear them arguing, but he didn't care. He needed one more lead before they shoved him off. He asked Beth to tell him every detail of the night she could recall, and he jotted them down as fast as they left her mouth. Then he asked the one question that had been bothering him all night.

"Where is Lilly's father? Is he the same father of the baby?"

"I don't know who Lilly's father is. I was young and dating a lot. He hasn't ever been in our lives, but I left my new baby's father two nights ago." She looked down as she spoke. "I had to do it. I couldn't let him hurt us anymore."

The doors to the ambulance flew open and the EMT's pulled at the gurney, yanking Beth from his grasp. Instinctively, Daniel knew she was trying to deceive him, and now he didn't have time to find out how or why.

Chapter 6

Detective Frank Martinez scanned the scene. He was looking for something more, something that would spiral the case in the right direction. As of that moment, nothing seemed right. He felt like he was spinning his wheels. There were no leads, just the words of a pregnant woman that didn't add up, some witnesses that didn't see a damn thing, and broken glass. He felt sure the mother was hiding something, and he was determined to figure out what.

The storm subsided, and the rain was now a slow, annoying trickle returning in intermittent spurts. The new day's light was still about an hour from illuminating the still spiteful sky, and he was hopeful a reluctant clue would surface somewhere. Another member of his team already asked for the surveillance tape from the diner, and based on the recap from the team member, the footage was pretty much nonexistent. Apparently, the manager thought simply having cameras up was enough of a security measure. The guy hadn't actually ever put in tapes because, in his words, "It was a waste of good money." So now Martinez felt exasperated. He reached for his cigarette pack and tapped one into his palm while he paced the lot. Anger burst through his body as he kicked an empty soda can that lay abandoned on the ground.

He searched the parking lot through worn-out eyes as he puffed on his second cigarette. Frank took several steps away from the diner into the bleak parking lot as he contemplated his next move, wondering if there really was one. His eyes slowly soaked in the scene. The Walgreen's across the street was well lit compared to the dingy little diner with its fake surveillance cameras. Even from the diner's parking lot, he could see the red blinking light from the cameras. Excitement bubbled under his skin as his adrenaline burst into overdrive.

He threw his lit cigarette down to the soggy ground, hearing it sizzle as the heat was snuffed out. Martinez ran across the street to the Walgreen's, a glimmer of hope filling him. His heart sank when he found the store appeared closed. He pulled on the door anyway, hoping to find them unlocked, but they didn't budge. A sign stated the place opened at 9:00 am. "Shit!" Frank exclaimed through clenched teeth. The exasperation grew from deep within. Instinctively, he reached for his cell, dialing Anna, his best go-to gal to get things done.

No one argued with Anna. She was a mean bitch when she needed to be, and as sweet as pie other times. He knew she'd do whatever it took to get the Walgreen's manager out of his or her cozy bed at 5 am simply because Anna told him to.

The phone rang once. Detective Martinez smiled coolly as he heard her voice on the other line. Victory would soon be his.

"Anna, it's Frank… yep. I have a favor."

After he explained his dilemma to Anna, he hung up his cell. A huge grin plastered his face. Frank walked out into the parking lot and checked the angle the cameras were placed and considered whether the wait would be worth it. Feeling satisfied this wasn't a completely lost cause, he decided to go back to the diner and grab some coffee while he waited. His mind drifted to his wife and how he wished he was lying next to her instead of walking alone in the damp morning air. Tomorrow would have been his first day off in weeks. He knew she would be disappointed to get his call, saying he couldn't come home any time soon. The diner's parking lot was bustling with activity as he passed through. He pulled the glass door open and nodded at a fellow officer as he passed him. A redheaded waitress greeted him with a grin when he approached the counter. He ordered his coffee to go and waited for her to get it for him. Feeling

like he hadn't heard from his partner in forever, he pulled out his cell

phone to check for missed calls. Finding none, he put it back in his

pocket. He was fighting the urge to pull out another smoke when the

waitress returned with his coffee. Smiling warmly, he thanked her

while he placed a five-dollar bill into her palm.

"Keep the change," he said as he took the lid off his cup and

ripped open six sugars, simultaneously pouring them into his coffee.

He followed the sugar with two creamers. Looking up briefly, he

caught the waitress trying to hide a sour grin that crossed her face.

"I like sugar." He picked up the spoon, giving his coffee a

good stir.

She grabbed a towel and wiped the already sparkling counter

as he replaced the lid, tapped the counter, nodded goodbye, and

turned on his heels. It was fifteen minutes tops when the disheveled

manager of Walgreen's showed up. The man was soft, and pudgy

with a horrible comb-over that covered a huge bald spot, but what

Frank appreciated the most was the gentleman's sense of urgency as

he departed his vehicle. He greeted the manager with a stern, non-

apologetic face. He smothered a snicker when he noticed the man was still wearing his flannel pajamas and slippers. *Good ol' Anna.* Frank could tell he had the upper hand, thanks to her, and he had no intention of losing it.

"So, these cameras you have here, do they work?" Frank asked as he jerked his head toward the camera above the door.

"Well, uhh… the last time I checked, they did. I have to go in around back. These doors will sound an alarm if they're opened," he said. He motioned with his shoulders as he walked past Frank toward the back of the Walgreen's. "Uhh, you can follow me around back and I'll get you in, and we can check out the tapes." The manager grabbed his keys by the ring and fumbled with them as he walked.

"I hope you actually put in tapes in yours." Martinez stated.

The pudgy man stopped short and turned to face him. His eyes pressed into slits, "What do you think, I'm an idiot?"

Frank smiled, something he tried not to do often, especially while he was working. He decided in that moment he actually liked the bald, fat guy, after all.

They reached the steel back door after several moments of walking in silence. The man played with the keys again, looking for the one that would unlock the door. His hand trembled as he twisted the key into the lock.

"This crime, you say happened at the diner?"

"Yes."

Opening the door and switching on a light, they stepped over the threshold and the balding man closed the door securely.

The manager turned his attention toward another door marked "Managers Only" and unlocked it. "Our cameras are pretty good, but I don't know how much you'll be able to see of the diner." He flipped on the lights in the office.

They entered the manager's office, and he walked over to the computer. Quickly, he flicked the outdated machine to life. The screen illuminated the room and a quiet buzzing filled the space. Within minutes, the list of footage time was displayed on the screen. His fingers sifted through the time frame for when the incident likely occurred. Before long, Beth's rusted green Malibu could be seen entering the diner's parking lot.

The manager was right. The footage wasn't great and unfortunately, she'd parked where a gigantic willow tree blocked most of the view. He could see her get out of the car, and pull her coat over her head as she fled toward the entrance of the diner, but there was no clear view of the little girl. What was clear was that within minutes of her entering the diner, a dark-colored van, possibly black, pulled up behind the car, completely blocking her car from view. No one reported seeing a black van, but there it was on the tape, not clear as day, but noticeable nonetheless. Frank could see one man emerge from the passenger side of the van. A moment passed, lightning flashed, and the footage flickered from visible to a complete fuzzy mess. He slammed his hand on the desk and leaned closer to the screen. There were four long seconds of shattered squiggly interference. When the footage snapped back into view Frank's mouth dropped open.

"What the hell?"

Chapter 7

Daniel was waiting outside the hospital room with a coffee cup in hand and his foot tapping anxiously on the floor. He couldn't wait to get inside to question her further. Given the circumstances, they expedited her to the top of the list in patient priority. They promised to let him speak to her as soon as they knew she was out of danger. He doubted that doctors even knew the definition of the word "quickly." With a sigh, he gave in to fatigue, and sat down in the chair they had placed next to him. He leaned forward, letting his head fall into his hands.

He hated waiting. Finally, he jolted upright and pulled his phone from his pocket. It displayed an animated envelope alerting him to a waiting text. His thoughts raced as he opened it, hoping it wasn't something important he'd missed.

It read, "At Walgreen's across from diner. Checking out surveillance video. Could be promising. Will update ASAP. When done, come find me."

Daniel clicked reply. "Okay. Promising?" Send.

He despised when his partner didn't elaborate, but he knew the reason why. Martinez never revealed too much unless he knew something for sure, and if it was crucial information, he would have called instead of texted. He closed his phone and put it back in his pocket before he leaned back in his seat and crossed his arms. His thoughts wandered. They were a first-rate team that provided a good balance for each other. Martinez was hot headed where Daniel was more even-tempered. He knew Martinez would energize him once they were reunited, but right now, Daniel was bone tired, and the investigation was only hours old. He lifted his coffee cup to his lips and growled when he found it empty. Looking around, he considered his options. He didn't want to leave his post, but he needed coffee badly.

Saving him from deliberation, the door to her room opened and two doctors emerged. The older of the two doctors dismissed the other with a gentle nod, and he turned to face Daniel.

"I'm Doctor. Stevens. I'll be the lead doctor on the case. In a situation like this, they appoint one doctor to be the go between for all allowed information." The doctor shrugged his shoulders as he tried to emphasize his next words. "That way, you'll always know

45

who to ask when you have a question. This also puts me on call for as long as she's here." The doctor paused.

He parted his feet and stood firmly, hinting he had a lot to say. "Mrs. Waters is stable. Based on the quick ultrasound, we believe she is about thirty-six weeks along. She did start having contractions, but we've been able to stop them." The doctor's hands stopped abruptly in mid motion and his posture shifted. "We hope to keep her from delivering for at least one more week." Sadness filled his eyes. "She hasn't had any prenatal care, so we want the baby to hold out as long as possible." His thumb lifted up to his brow, and he gave it a thoughtful scratch. "Typically, we can only keep her overnight, and depending on how she does, we will release her tomorrow morning," he added with a loud exhale.

Doctor Stevens folded his arms over his chest and eyed the detective curiously. "I do have some questions for you before I'll answer any questions you may have for me, though. Do you mind?"

Daniel shifted his weight and rested his hands on his hips, feeling annoyed, but he decided to keep it in check. He needed this doctor's cooperation. "No."

The doctor took a step away from the door, closing the distance between them.

Daniel was trained to detect a change in human behavior and analyze it. It was a passion he'd developed through his time dealing with criminals. He enjoyed trying to figure out people based on what their hidden languages told him. Right now, he was getting the message the doctor was worried about something, and Daniel desperately wanted to know what. He also doubted the man would actually say what he was worried about outright.

"Do you know if Mrs. Waters…err Beth, has been in an accident that you know of?"

The question hit Daniel like a thud to the gut. "No, not that I know of. Why? Do you think she has?" Prescott let the questions fly unapologetically from his mouth. His mind was reeling at the implications behind the doctor's inquiry. His hand fumbled with the empty coffee cup as he waited for a response.

"Well, and I'm going to speak frankly with you, as I examined this lady, everything checks out fine. She seems completely healthy. Her blood pressure, her weight, her blood sugar level, everything appears okay, with the consideration of typical pregnancy issues, and yet I'm feeling there's something off. Now it could just be the trauma of losing her child, and possibly a little bit of shock. And to be honest with you, only time will reveal what's normal for her psychologically, but this is my gut feeling." The doctor sighed. "I shouldn't be bringing my gut into this. To be straightforward with you, though, my inner feeling tells me there is more to it. Like long term PTSD. I might be missing something. I just don't know yet what it is." The doctor shoved his hands stiffly into his white coat pockets as he weighed his next words. "If she has been in an accident or suffered some kind of additional trauma, it will explain some of her behavior and lack of information."

Daniel mulled over the new discovery. He wasn't quite sure what to make of any of it, but he did remember she mentioned having to get away from the unborn child's father. His mind did a mental rewind to something the doctor said earlier.

"Doctor, what do you mean by normal pregnancy issues? In regards to Mrs. Waters, what is it you could be missing, if anything?"

"To be honest, a pregnancy can wreak havoc on a woman's body. You'd think that it's a completely normal condition, but no two pregnant women are the same. For example, I've had pregnant patients who had perfect vision before they're pregnant, that end up needing glasses while pregnant. That is a mild variance, though." His hands were moving once again as he threw emphasis into his statements. "I've had women who show up completely normal throughout their pregnancy and suddenly something chemically happens within their bodies that throws them into seizures, sometimes even a coma, and there is no explanation for it." His fingers rested on his brow. Daniel watched the doctor as he visibly processed the information. With a shrug, the doctor continued. "As an OBGYN doctor, it's like walking on uncharted territory all the time. You never really know what to expect from one patient to the next."

Satisfied the doctor was finished speaking, Daniel decided to probe for more. "What does that mean for Mrs. Waters?" He brushed his hands through his dirty blonde hair. "I mean, to be honest with you, I don't know what you're telling me." He audibly sighed, letting his exasperation show. His arms folded across his chest while his right hand found its way up to his mouth, where a finger rubbed the stubble that was beginning to show on his upper lip.

49

Thoughtfully, he considered what the doctor was trying to explain to him.

The doctor played with his stethoscope; his apprehension was obvious. "That's just it. I really don't know. I'm not an expert on head trauma. The physical sings aren't there, but the psychological signs are. It's going to take a lot of time to figure her out. The hospital won't let her stay unless she's in danger, and all the tests say she's not." He took a few steps to his left and back again. "Because the tests don't show anything and you say she hasn't had any kind of head trauma or recent injury, I have no reason to push to keep her, although I'd like to." He paused briefly. "I just feel I need to. If I could keep her, I could analyze her more and maybe find something that's amiss, but given what I know and what you know, I won't be able to. Legally, my hands are tied." He stressed the word 'legally.' He dropped his arms to his side in defeat. "The only thing I can suggest, Detective, is that you keep a close eye on her once she's discharged. I'll give you my card so we can be in touch. I'll do my best to figure out what I can."

Daniel came into the hospital confused and now he'd leave even more confused. The doctor's words seemed to crush him from the outside in. *Just what the hell was going on in Moore, Oklahoma?* How could it be possible a child can go missing and a pregnant woman can leave two highly qualified men baffled? He knew this case was going to either kill him, or turn him grey before his time, but there was no turning away. No way in hell. It was his job to see this through. He extended his hand to Dr. Stevens in gratitude.

"Thank you, doctor. I'll take your card, and you better believe I'll call you." He gave a slight smile as he took the card, placing it securely into his wallet. "May I go in now? I do have some more questions for her, unless there is more we need to discuss now."

"Go right ahead. I don't have anything else as of right now."

"Thank you. I'll be in touch."

Daniel watched as the man turned to leave. He felt relieved about the doctor's candid approach, but dumbfounded by his revelations. Feeling jumbled caused doubt to creep in.

Before he entered the room, a uniformed officer arrived to take his post by Mrs. Waters' room. He was relieved to see him arrive. He wanted to be sure this mother, AKA victim, AKA suspect, would be highly guarded every second, especially given the new

information or lack thereof shed on the situation.

***

Daniel gave a gentle knock on room 243. The voice within

invited him to enter. He pushed past the thick white curtains that

circled over the opening in front of the door. Beth turned her gaze

downward when she saw him. Her hands twisted on the rough

hospital sheet that covered her bulging abdomen. A faint smile

passed over her face. He could tell it was more for his comfort than

for hers. Her body looked even weaker than the last time he saw her,

but behind her dull, light brown eyes, he could see a thick layer of

strength still residing within. He was relieved. She'd need all the

strength she could get if she was going to face the next few days.

"Did you miss me?" Daniel joked, trying to lighten the

tension-filled air separating them. It seemed to work. Her tepid smile

grew in warmth. Pulling up a chair, he took a seat by her side,

allowing a soothing smile to form across his face. He watched as her

eyes followed his moves. Slowly, he slid back in the chair and pulled

52

his ankle up and let it rest on the opposite knee. Beth rose up straighter in bed. "Detective…did you find her?"

His heart sunk. He wanted desperately to tell her yes. He wanted to be the good news bearer she was wishing for, but he wasn't. Not yet anyway.

"No. Ma'am, we're working on it, but right now, we don't have any leads. We need you to shove us in the right direction." He stood up and crossed to the window. Twisting the blinds closed with a snap of his wrist, he turned and sat back down in his chair. He knew from experience that the morning light from the east would shine directly in her eyes if the blinds were left open.

"We've put out an Amber alert, and her picture is plastered all over the news," Prescott informed the woman. "We don't have her yet, though. We would like to…. you have no idea how badly we'd like to." He smiled without conviction. He was really trying. Hell, they all were. His tired body leaned forward in his seat and he allowed his chin to rest on his closed fist while he thought about the grief she must be feeling.

The young lady in the bed seemed to detect his self-doubt with her eyes. He could feel her will and determination pour out of her. Then her face stiffened as anger washed over her, covering her in scarlet blotches.

"Listen here, detective, you get that sappy, good for nothing look off of your face. You will find my little girl for me if it takes your last breath." Anger sparked in her eyes. "Do you hear me? I won't take no for an answer." She violently twisted her bed sheet.

All Daniel could do was watch and listen. He felt like a schoolboy caught cheating on a test. Daniel let his gaze fall to the floor as he took in the scolding. He knew she was right, and shame filled him for one fleeting moment and then recharged him. His feet tapped on the tiled floor as the energy began to pulse through his veins. Slowly, he let his eyes face her again. *Good for you, Beth. Give us some spunk, help us out here.* A sensation of hope pushed his doubt to the side. He stifled the smile that wanted to escape his lips.

"Someone out there has her and you will find her," she continued, fire blazed from her eyes. "You can't tell me she just vanished into thin air. That just doesn't happen."

Her finger stiffly pointed at him; unseen threats darted from it like daggers. "It won't happen to my Lilly. You hear me, detective? Her name is Lilly. You need to recognize that. She was there, singing to me, and then she was gone, but she was there, in that diner, with me, and you will figure out who took her. Do you hear me, detective?" she paused and sucked in a breath. "Because, if you can't find her, then you need to tell me now, and I will. I'm not going to sit here feeling scared, putting my faith in you if you can't get the job done."

A moment ago, he was excited about her newfound strength, and now he stared at her in disbelief. Where was all this coming from? One minute the scared victim, the next a cougar. She was scolding him like his own mother would have, and he had to admit right then, in that moment, he liked it. It was just the kick in the behind he needed. It was the faith renewing feeling he desired. Daniel was impressed with the woman's articulate, bossy nature. He knew he needed to consider her as a suspect; and he would, but he felt sure she'd kick his ass if he didn't pull through his self-doubt and solve her case. He let his smile plaster its genuine form across his face. "All right then, Beth. Let's find her." He quickly pulled out his pocket size notebook again ready to take notes. "I need to ask a few more questions. Are you up to it?"

Beth released the sheet and attempted to flatten it on her belly. "I might be pregnant, detective, but I can handle whatever it takes to find my Lilly." She crossed her arms over her chest.

"All right then, let's begin." He pulled out his pen and grinned. "I'm going to get straight to the point. I'm going to ask all the hard questions first. I'm going to piss you off, but you will answer every question without holding back, and with complete honesty." He emphasized his words boldly. Allowing his eyes to dart a warning as he locked his onto hers, he pointed his finger firmly in her direction. "Don't lie to me about anything." *If she faltered in any way, she'd remain his number one suspect,* he thought as he prepared for his first question. "Those are my terms." He let his brown eyes scorch through her the same way hers did only moments before. "If you fail me, then I'll walk out of here. I'll go to the media, and I'll name you as our only suspect. Is that clear, Mrs. Waters?" Prescott stunned himself with his threatening approach, but for some reason he felt she would approve.

She stared at him and her eyes glassed over with tears. "I'd expect nothing less, detective."

The young mother answered each of his questions with honesty, as far as he could tell. There were moments when he had to wait for her to stop sobbing, and times when anger shook the room, but through it all, he remained straight faced and unbiased. Being impartial was a duty he performed well most of the time.

She retold everything he already knew, and now he wanted to know more. He wanted to know where her story began. The next subject was the father. Who was he? Where was he? And did he have a role in the situation? He recalled his promise to Martinez to drill her on the baby daddy subject. Unfortunately, this is where things got hazy and soiled with uncertainty. This is where her answers lacked detail and omitting details was an issue with Daniel. It suggested a suspect was hiding something, and he wasn't happy.

"I left him."

"Why?"

"Because he was no good."

"How so?"

"He was abusive. He didn't want us."

"So, you left him...when?"

"Yes. Two nights ago, I think. It's all a blur."

"Blur? You think you left him two nights ago? Beth, I need to know an exact time frame. Leaving your baby's father seems like a major event. I don't believe you don't remember. You're lying to me and making me dig, and I don't like it." He set his jaw firmly and sat back in his chair with folded his arms tightly across his chest.

Red flags were popping up all over. If Martinez were here, he wouldn't ask another question. He would've gotten right in her face and screamed at her. But he wasn't here. Daniel was. He needed to find a way to get the information.

"I told you; it was all a blur. It happened so fast," replied Beth finally.

"Explain to me in detail what you remember the night you left," Daniel asked coolly. He tapped his pencil against the notebook and stared her down.

Beth took a deep breath and closed her eyes. "It was Friday night. I'd been thinking for some time about leaving him. He didn't know I was planning to go. It was stormy outside, like last night. He'd been drinking all day, and bad weather always put him in a nasty mood."

The detective took notes as he watched her, and he noticed the pain etched on her face. Her body seemed to shrink into the hospital bed until she looked like a child shivering under the sheet. It pained him to watch her, but he dared not interrupt the flow. He could sense she was sinking into a world all her own and that's exactly where he wanted her. That world was where the truth waited.

"I was washing the dishes. Lilly was playing under the sink. She likes to play under the sink when I'm washing the dishes. She's kind of funny that way."

Daniel watched in awe as a spark returned to her spirit. A smile crept across his face.

"She's like my shadow, following me everywhere."

A soft glow of happiness surfaced on her face in tiny pink blotches under her skin whenever she mentioned Lilly. Then, as soon as she'd recall details about the father of the baby, the happiness would turn into a dark shadow of shame and sorrow under her eyes. He listened intently, taking notes on details and reflecting on the words she didn't say when she spoke, the words her eyes and body said instead. He was grateful for the classes he took about the secret messages of body language, which at the time seemed silly and unnecessary. He didn't say a word as she told her story.

"He was going on and on about how he didn't want us. He always did that when he was mad. I had become numb to his words." Her lips thinned, and the color drained from them as she spoke of the hate she felt for this man. Daniel could tell she was about to share a painful detail, and he braced himself for it.

"Then, before long, he came up behind me. He didn't say anything. He just kind of stood there breathing and taunting me with his presence," she recalled. "The booze reeked on his breath. It was disgusting," she added with great distaste. "He grabbed my hair and yanked me back." Beth's face contorted as the memory spilled from her mouth. Her hands swayed through the motions of her tale, twisting the sheet tightly again. Her knuckles turned white from the strain. "I remember feeling my belly hit the counter. Pain shot through me and I worried about the baby."

She stopped speaking briefly, and a tear ran down her cheek, landing in a salty pool that grew right above her abdomen. She smothered her grief-stricken face with her hands. He'd seen that look many times. He felt shameful because all he wanted was for her to get past that moment and continue with her story. He didn't know if she'd continue, but before he had a chance to call for a break, she went on.

"Then, he said he was done with me and he was going to kill me right then and there. He dragged me back by my hair so hard I fell to the floor. He yanked on me, dragging me from the kitchen." She stopped briefly as she motioned with her hands. "I could see Lilly peeking out from under the sink. She was so scared, but she wasn't making a fuss. I was so proud of her for not making a sound. If she did, then he would've found her and hurt her, too. She was such a good girl."

She gave another pause as she caught her breath before she continued her story. Her hands gently caressed her neck where Daniel spied a tiny bruise.

"Then he got on top of me. He was sitting on my belly, and he didn't even care he was squashing the baby. He grabbed me by the throat and squeezed hard. I thought my neck might break. It hurt so badly." She squinted as she recalled the pain from that night. "I was kicking and fighting the best I could, but I was no match for him. I managed to hit him in the nuts one good time, and it pissed him off something fierce." Daniel noticed a small twist near her mouth that indicated she was quite proud of having hurt the guy.

"He hit me here real hard after that." She motioned to the side of her head. "I thought I was going to black out then and there, but I didn't. He was still recovering from the blow to the groin. He was kind of chuckling like some kind of psycho and he was about to come at me again when I saw his rifle leaning against the wall just within my reach. I grabbed it and swung it forward as hard as I could. I hit him square on the head. Then he fell to the floor, out cold."

She looked up and stared straight into the detective's eyes before she continued.

"I wanted to shoot the piece of shit, but I couldn't. It was in that moment I knew I had to leave. I tied him up with the phone cord and I grabbed Lilly, some clothes, and we fled. I didn't look back. I was afraid to. I'm not ever going back there again, either," she stated firmly as she crossed her arms, indicating there was no negotiation about that idea.

Daniel sat in quiet awe. It sickened him to know there was a man twisted enough to beat a pregnant woman like that. The information placed the bastard straight to the top of his list of suspects. He stared at the small bruise on her neck, in the spot she'd caressed while retelling the story, but it wasn't a significant mark. He'd seen some horrible bruises on people who claimed to be strangled. There was no way to tell if it actually happened or not.

"Beth, what is his name? Where can we find him?" He'd been dying to ask her that question, but he didn't want to stop her from telling her story.

"Do you have to know that information, detective? If he finds me, he'll kill me." She looked at the Daniel pleadingly.

He looked her squarely in the eye before he replied. "Your face and name are plastered all over the news everywhere. If we don't find him, he'll find you," he stated firmly.

Chapter 8

Frank was getting increasingly agitated with the situation. That damn lightning had ruined the most crucial part of the footage. Right now, the manager of Walgreen's was trying to recover the few seconds lost on the video. While he was working on that, Frank went shopping through the dark store. He needed a boost of energy. His nerves were on fire from the adrenaline rush. Frank knew it wouldn't be long before his mind would rebound and turn into a ball of mush. He kept replaying what he thought he saw on the footage to no avail. It made no sense. He had to be sure. He needed that footage desperately.

He loaded up his arms with energy drinks and Doritos, and then threw them into a tiny red basket. His wife would kill him if she knew he was snacking on this kind of crap, but he didn't care. That's what he told himself, anyway. Feeling pleased with his purchase, he headed back to the office. Before he reached it, he heard a loud tap on the storefront window. Turning, he found Daniel peering through the glass at him. About time he showed up! Frank motioned and mouthed with exaggeration for his partner to meet him at the back door. Then he turned back toward the back entry.

Now he could get this shit figured out. That manager better get that damn footage fixed! Cursing under his breath, he passed the office to open the back door for Daniel.

Once the door was open and his partner stepped in, Frank carelessly tossed a Red Bull into his arms, which nearly ended up on the floor.

"Where have you been? Did 'Mommy Dearest' give up anything?"

Daniel grinned at him. "I got some good information, but nothing that will lead us anywhere yet. She can't remember much past yesterday." Daniel brushed his hands through his hair. "She's refusing to give up the father's name right now, too." He held up his hands before Frank could start in. "I'm working on it, though. I hope you have something," he added as they stepped in front of the office, which was illuminated with a dull overhead light and a computer screen.

Frank gave his partner "the" look. "What the hell do you mean 'can't remember' and not giving up his name? Is she stupid?"

There was nothing that bothered Frank more than thick people who wouldn't know help if it slapped them across the face.

"I don't know. It's a real long story. I'll catch you up," he shrugged as they stepped inside the office for a better view of the computer screen. "What's this promising footage you said you have?"

Frank leaned toward his partner and whispered, "Okay, so get this. The footage needs to be recovered before I can say for sure, but I think I saw something." Frank explained about the black van, and how curiously it appeared just after Beth entered the diner. "I believe there were two people, possibly men," he added. "It's too far away, and too dark to know for sure. The man in the passenger side facing us got out of the van, and walked to the opposite side, near where the victim's car was. He was Caucasian, wearing dark clothes. I can't make out any features, though." He popped the cap on his Red Bull, sending hisses of vapor escaping from the can in a gentle swoosh. He raised the can to his lips and paused. "I also can't tell for sure about the gender, but it looks like a man. With some work on the tapes, we should be able to determine that. Pajama Man here said he might be able to recover some of it." He motioned toward the

66

Walgreen's manager, who glanced momentarily at the two detectives before he focused back on the screen. "I'm hoping he can zoom in some on the plate, but I don't know if he can. It's killing me, Daniel." He swiped his hand across his face as if that would wipe some of the frustration away. Frank leaned in closer to his partner. "I saw the back of the van open up and I can't be sure, but I think the fucker put something in the back of it." His last words revealed the final details he had to share with Daniel, but the shock value they supplied to the moment hung between them like a big gaping hole.

Daniel's eyes flew open wide with surprise. "What! Can you tell what it is?"

"Shit, no. I can't even be sure I saw that. The damn storm wigged out the freaking tape. I don't know if I actually saw it, or if I just imagined that I did. That's why I'm so on edge. We need that tape!" He shrugged and motioned in the direction of the diner. "That piece of shit across the street doesn't even have tapes in his damn camera, so this crap here is all we have to work with."

Frank watched as Daniel popped open his Red Bull and took a large gulp. Frank set his on the desk. He placed the bag of Nacho Doritos down as well and produced a twenty-dollar bill from his wallet. He set the money down in front of the manager and considered his energy meal more than paid for. He turned his attention back to his partner. Frank could see the thoughts and questions swirling behind his squinty, puppy-like brown eyes.

Before Daniel could ask more questions, the manager spoke, cutting the silence with his words. "I think that's as good as it's going to get right now. Would you like to see it?" he asked as he punched one final key on the keyboard and swiveled the computer screen. The two detectives stepped forward, leaning into the screen for a closer look as the manager pressed play. The night's event replayed in a fuzzy haze across the screen. The manager slowed time when the van emerged behind Beth's car, causing each second to last longer. It was agonizing to watch and wait. Time itself, if passed in vain, can be a punisher of the innocent who wait. Then, quite suddenly it felt like time stopped all together. It felt like they'd been swallowed by its evil presence.

Frank was right. He did see the back of the van open up. He also saw someone put something in the back of the van. But what? The tape clicked off before the van door closed. Could it have been

Lilly? The detectives looked at each other. Their mouths uttering the same.

"Son of a bitch."

They were dealing with two criminals and they definitely put something into the back of the van.

Chapter 9

Daniel smacked his hand down on the desk. He was pissed. They didn't have enough clues yet. He stared blankly at the screen, hoping it would come back with something more to go on, but it didn't. Slowly, he bowed his head and shook it back and forth in disgust. His blood boiled as anger filled him. A phone book lay within his grasp. His rage exploded as he grabbed it with one hand and threw it against the wall. It fell in a dissatisfying thud against the floor. Without a plate or a name, they had nothing. He turned briefly to Frank.

"Calm down there, cowboy. You're the levelheaded one, remember?" Frank winked at him. "We'll get this son of a bitch."

He turned away from Frank. He wasn't ready to calm down and frustration sizzled in the back of his eyes as he glared at the Walgreen's manager. He lurched toward him with one finger pointing like a dagger in his face.

"We can't release this footage." It wasn't a statement, but instead, a command. "If we do, then whoever is in that van will know we're on to them. Do you understand me?" His face was inches away from the man in pajamas standing in front of him. The manager was nodding his head furiously. "I'm not kidding," Daniel spat. "We have a lead, not a great lead, but a lead nonetheless, so if you go running your mouth off to the media, then we'll lose any chance we have of finding this little girl. Are we clear?" Daniel hated using scare tactics to make a point, but he never let his pride refuse to interfere when necessary. Tonight, it was essential, and he'd never apologize for the discomfort he was causing the man who stood in front of him.

The manager stammered, "Yeah, yeah, I get it. I won't release the tape. I, err...might be able to help some more," he added cautiously.

The two detectives said nothing as they waited for him to elaborate further. In unison, they folded their arms across their chests and stubbornly widened their stances. The fingers of the right hand of each detective tapped expectantly. The manager would never know how they had practiced that move for months to get it just right. The partners gave each other a lifted eyebrow as they watched Pajama Man hurry to the computer screen and hit some keys which caused the screen to zoom lower, bringing the van's blurry plate into view. Daniel took two curious steps forward and peered over the guy's shoulder while he worked.

"It has an Arkansas plate." Pajama Man pointed at the screen. "You can't see Arkansas on the top of the plate because of the angle, but if you look at the bottom, you can see the word 'Natural State'. Arkansas has the logo, 'The Natural State', on many of their plates."

He pointed above the words to the blurry numbers and continued slowly, "I can take a copy of the tape home," he paused, his next words crushed by the detective's ominous glare. He threw his hands up, waving off their suspicion. "No…No. Just hear me out. I'm a computer geek," he explained quickly. "I was just going to offer to enhance it at home and see if I can get the plate. I have a much better computer setup at home."

Frank waved him off, silencing the fidgety man. "Look, I know you think working with us is going to somehow make your life more interesting, and maybe your wife will actually want to sleep with you again, but we have computer geeks of our own. Thanks, but no thanks. We will be taking this baby with us. Swear to shut up about this and let us take it from here. If our geeks can't get the job done, we'll call you." Frank slapped the guy on the back and gave him an all too serious look. A smile of pure admiration grew on his face. "That Natural Arkansas shit was actually pretty impressive," he grinned. "I think I might kiss you right now, you know that?"

The man took a step back. "Nah. I'm just kidding. I won't kiss you." He gave the manager a firm pat on the chest.

Despite how wired Daniel was feeling, he couldn't help but smirk at his partner right now. Frank was trying to be a hard ass with the poor guy, but Daniel could tell Frank actually liked him. Daniel would place money on it. He knew Frank all too well. It didn't happen all that often, but when Frank liked someone, they became his lifelong friend. The cranky detective seemed to save places in his heart for people of value. Daniel found it an admirable trait. The manager didn't know it yet, but he was building a lifelong friendship with a man who would take a bullet for him. So as of right now, Daniel was going to let his friend play the hard ass card all he wanted.

***

The manager made a copy of the tape as requested, and the detectives gave him their cards and then left. They entered into his life much like the storm, uninvited and forceful. He clasped his

73

hands together to keep them from shaking. He couldn't believe he was doing this, but he knew he could clean up that tape. He slipped the original into his robe pocket, locked up and called in sick from his cell phone as he hurried to his car. He didn't know how good the department "geeks" were, but he did know how good he was. He'd been a geek his whole life, and now was the time to make it count for something.

Chapter 10

Beth sat in her hospital bed. The sun had already permeated through the edges of her curtains and her mind, reminding her life does go on, even when you don't want it to. Her eyes burned as the sun moved across the room. She hadn't slept well, regardless of the sleep aids they gave her. Her dreams were troubled with images of Lilly's feet as they danced under the bathroom stall. The memory of the moment haunted her. She couldn't count how many times she'd woken from her fitful slumber as Lilly's voice echoed through her broken mind. Beth wanted desperately to join the search. Time was passing her by and it was taking Lilly with it.

Beth rose from her bed. She felt the need to get her body moving. In the bathroom, her mind wandered. She couldn't help but question if she was causing more damage by not revealing her boyfriend's name. She felt certain in the moment when the detective asked, but now she was second guessing her decision. Beth felt strongly it wasn't him. Silently she hoped he was dead, or dying slowly from starvation. Men like him didn't deserve to breathe, but he wouldn't want Lilly. She would just be in his way.

Even if he'd gotten free after they fled, there was no way in hell he would have known where to find her, she reasoned. Neither of them had been to Oklahoma together, ever, and when she left, she took the only vehicle he had. He never even registered the vehicle in their names, so she knew even the car couldn't be traced. She didn't want the detectives wasting time looking for her boyfriend when someone else had Lilly. Her confidence was high in that regard. Lying was the only way she could think to help Lilly faster. She needed to keep the detectives from going off on some kind of tangent and looking in the wrong place.

It crushed her when she looked in Detective Prescott's eyes and saw the disappointment her lies caused, but she wasn't trying to please him. She was trying to save her daughter. Beth knew it angered him, and she was feeling guilty about it, but it was for the good of Lilly.

She didn't care if Detective Prescott thought she was an idiot, or hiding something. The way she saw it, if withholding that information kept them away from Arkansas and her stupid boyfriend, then she was doing right by her Lilly; even if keeping her secret meant her boyfriend would find her like the detective suggested.

She splashed water on her face and checked her image in the mirror. The hours that passed aged her. Her hair was a raging mess. Beth wasn't vain, but when she looked at her reflection in the mirror, she was shocked. Her shoulder length hair was a frizzed mess. Her light chocolate eyes were aged by grief and her lips were dry and cracked. The sight of her own image frightened her. She placed her hand on the mirror as if the action would dispel the pitiful creature in the reflection and closed her eyes. When she opened them, the worn-out reflection remained. It taunted her. It accused her. She couldn't face the image a moment longer. Walking away, she closed the bathroom door, hoping to imprison all the wretchedness within.

Beth hated hospitals. She couldn't remember the last time she was in one, but she hated them. Her fingers traced across her brow as she thought; she couldn't even remember her hospital stay when Lilly was born. At first, the thought startled her, but she shrugged it away. She didn't want to try to remember right now. It wasn't important.

Her feet lazily carried her across the cold floor, hauling her toward the window almost against her will. She needed to see the world, and yet she didn't want to see it. *Did it continue to revolve aimlessly?* she wondered as she opened the curtain and pulled the string raising the blinds. The sun insulted her eyes. She squinted as the rays burned to her soul. Her view was from several stories up and overlooked a parking lot.

Down below, she could see dozens of people. They were standing there holding signs. The sight intrigued her. She wondered what they were doing. It wasn't long before one of the signs became clear to her. It was an image of Lilly. The same image she'd given to the detective. Outside of her mind, it was the only image that remained of her little girl.

It was then Beth understood the assembly down below was for her. They were all gathered in hopes of spotting her. The idea of onlookers made her sick. She hoped her life wouldn't become a media sideshow. Perhaps they thought their presence was comforting? She gazed across the parking lot and noticed the news vans parked alongside the perimeter. Their company was portentous. A wave of nausea crashed against the wall of her stomach, causing her knees to weaken. This was all real. This was now her life. She knew every day this would be her reality, and she hated the thought. She tried to back away from the window, but her presence didn't go unnoticed.

Beth saw the fingers of the onlookers eagerly pointing up towards her. They accused her with knowing glances. They hated her. They pitied her. She could feel them. Hating. Loving. Pitying. Questioning. All of them just stared, and in the moments following their pointing, flashes of light revealed cameras trying to document that moment in time. She didn't know what to do. She didn't know how to feel. She didn't want to feel. Beth tried to deny all intrusions into her soul. She felt their shouts through the solid walls. Like poison arrows through her heart. Pain flashed through her head.

She wanted Lilly. The sorrow and loss crushed her to the floor. She fell in silence and wept as she curled up into a ball. She wept for her past. She wept for her present, and she wept for her future, and the entire unknown that penetrated her mind. The words, "What have I done?" stuttered from her mouth before she collapsed into the same familiar darkness that found her earlier.

Chapter 11

Back at the station, Daniel and Frank gave an overview of what they knew so far to the chief. A black cargo van was at the scene. Someone, possibly a white man and an assumed but never actually seen accomplice, put something in the back of the van. The van was most likely from Arkansas. That information was pending further investigation. They'd alert the Arkansas State Troopers to be on the lookout for such a vehicle, just in case.

The mother said she left on Friday. It was now Sunday morning. It was almost two days later. This information baffled the detectives. If she came from Arkansas, she could have come from just over the state line, or from well across the state. It depended on which route she chose to travel, and if she stopped a lot. They suspected she stopped often due to her driving with a child, and considering how pregnant she was. They were anxiously awaiting a definite location through plate identification, but it could take hours or even days for their computer technician to figure that out, if they're ever able to figure it out.

The mother was still being fully guarded by the city's finest, but she was also still refusing to give the name of her boyfriend. The chief sat and considered all the information presented to him. They had nothing to go on. He sat with his index fingers pressed over his top lip, thinking of what he should tell them. His lip was just beginning to show signs of gray stubble. It'd been well over ten hours since he'd last been home. His slate-blue eyes were downcast toward his desk as he swiveled gently in his chair. There was crap coming in from the Amber alerts. There were so many crazy people out there. Some of them were crazy enough to accuse their own mothers of taking the little girl. Hell, half of the state's force was out checking on what would no doubt end up being false leads. He felt stuck, and didn't know which direction to turn his boys loose. What he did know was, before long, the investigation would be invaded.

Since they'd most likely find the van from Arkansas, the jurisdiction and investigation would primarily be turned over to the FBI. He didn't like that. Not that he didn't want the case solved, but his men had made connections, and in some ways, progress. He didn't want their work undone. He wanted his men at the head of the game and one step ahead of the FBI, so he wasn't going to waste any of their time keeping them in the office. The FBI was already about to invade his office as it was, and that would no doubt cause a delay due to briefing procedures. He raised his head and looked at his detectives, who sat waiting for him. The sunlight beamed in the office, illuminated the dust in the air, and reminded him that daylight was burning.

"I want you guys to do what you do best. Go. Do what you need to do. Don't bother coming in unless you think you need to." He stood up and walked around to the side of his desk, folded his arms, and sat on the edge before he continued. "Call me to make your reports and keep pushing forward. I'll have a tech report for you as soon as they have something. Build a relationship with the mother," he suggested. "If she gets discharged, she'll need a place to stay. I'll make arrangements with Anna." He stood, placing a confident hand on Frank, who sat closest to him.

The fondness he felt for his officers was immeasurable. He'd spent fifteen years leading the department, and he'd seen officers come and go. There was an attachment he held for each one. They were his family. Their wives, husbands and children were all his to watch grow and achieve. The chief felt such sadness in recent days

82

as he watched the faith of the men sitting in front of him begin to waiver. He knew they needed this case to end well, and he prayed it would. If it didn't, then it would change things for the worse in the department. His family might disintegrate around him. He needed to cut the cord and let his men handle this case the way he knew they could.

"Anna is good at making anyone talk, even if they don't have anything to say." The chief gave a sigh. Having no leads or a known direction to turn is a crushing feeling. It's not a position you ever want to be in, in police work anyway. Anna no longer worked at the department, so the FBI wouldn't invade her right away. It would gain them a head start on the investigation.

Daniel and Frank nodded and left. The chief watched them, feeling proud. The years he'd put into their training would finally come to a head. His heart felt suddenly lighter, but he knew a huge part of his burden had walked out of the room and onto the shoulders of two of his bravest men. It was a burden he needed to pass on, though. He was nearing the end of his lead, and he had to decide who would sit in his chair.

***

After the meeting with the chief, Daniel felt compelled to call Dr. Stevens. The doctor asked before if Beth had been in an accident or suffered any head trauma. At the time, Daniel didn't know, but he remembered Beth saying something about being hit in the head in the struggle with her boyfriend. He felt certain that was worth telling the doctor. She also was strangled and Daniel felt certain a lack of oxygen for any period of time was worth mentioning as well.

Frank offered to make the call for him. He wanted to put a voice to the doctor's name. As Frank dialed the doctor, Daniel stepped into the technician's office to see if there had been any discoveries, or rather, recoveries of information.

He found the room bustling with activity. The computers buzzed and beeped with life. Daniel recalled his mandatory training in the computer lab. The department wanted each officer to know what it took to work behind the scenes, in what he'd considered the grunt work. Those ten hours convinced him he didn't ever want to work with computers. He hated the nagging noises, the constant beeping, and chatter from the irritating machines. He disliked being stuck in an office all day and the lab was worse than an office. It felt

84

like he was being suffocated. The respect he held for people who found this kind of job enjoyable was immense. He'd never agree with them, but he respected and appreciated them none the less.

"So, Marcus, how's it going?" Daniel inquired as he approached the man who Frank termed his personal computer 'geek.'

Marcus looked up from the screen as his hand continued to dance across the keys, punching in numbers and words. "The angle is bad, which you already know. We should be able to get out a few numbers for sure. We can cross reference those numbers with the type of van it is and see what comes up." Marcus threw himself back in his seat and folded his arms. "Once we have the matches, we'll eliminate females. We've been able to determine the suspect is a man based on body measurements and posture," he clarified as he turned back to the screen.

"So, do you have a time frame when that should be done?" Daniel knew asking that question was more of a formality. The answer would be unknown. He knew from experience computers were fantastic tools, but a job like this could take hours or even days. All he could do at this point was cross his fingers and hope today, of all days, the computer would be quick, and the matches would be few.

Marcus didn't even bother with a response. He just smiled up at Daniel, who knowingly grinned before he walked away, giving Marcus a pat on the back as he went.

"You know how to find me if something comes up," said Daniel.

"Yep."

That was all Daniel heard before the doors swung closed behind him, drowning out the humming from within the lab.

He found his partner just getting off of his cell phone outside the tech doors.

"So that was the good doctor. Anna is going to the hospital in about an hour to pick up Beth. She has agreed to stay with Anna while the investigation is pending. The doctor has released her only because she'll be with Anna." He paused thoughtfully, "Apparently, the bump on the head and lack of oxygen is a valid concern, but not enough of a reason to keep her since it's already been over twelve hours. Also, it sounds as if she passed out again," Frank stated in exasperation. "They found her on the floor of her room singing a song. The doctor said he's scheduling a psych evaluation. They'll send the shrink to Anna's. He said Beth seemed bothered by the media circus at the hospital and he felt she might do better away from the press." Both men turned to walk downstairs.

Frank continued his explanation. "They're going to have a nurse stop in every six hours to check on her for twenty-four hours as a precaution. Once they know more about her mental state, they'll decide where she needs to be, but for now, they want her as comfortable as possible for the sake of the baby."

Daniel felt relief knowing Beth would be with Anna, but frustrated knowing they couldn't keep her under medical watch in a hospital, at least for a few more hours.

The detectives walked the rest of the way out of the station in silence. There's no feeling more helpless than the feeling of not knowing.

Chapter 12

Beth was curious about Anna, but she didn't ask any questions when they said she'd be released to her care. She didn't want to be in a hospital anymore. Being released to Anna felt equivalent to being freed from a prison where your mind is tortured by the mere thought of captivity. Her mind was already slipping away from her, and she didn't like it. She hadn't felt this way for a long time.

They brought Beth out of a delivery entrance to avoid the press. Detective Prescott and Martinez were her escorts. Anna drove with the Hispanic detective next to her in the front seat. Beth and Detective Prescott were placed in the back of the SUV. She didn't know where they were going, and she didn't care. She was weak and tired.

She slumped down in her seat and stared out the passenger window. It angered her to see life moving so normally. The homeless were still homeless, and pitiful, begging for money. Commuters still drove aimlessly through the streets on the same path to success, or a lack thereof. Mothers were still mothers, pushing their children down the street in their strollers. Babies still cried and children played. Seeing children playing caused a crushing pain to fill her heart. She couldn't help but wish she'd see Lilly, perhaps holding the hand of some stranger. Silently, she imagined what it would feel like if she did. What would she do? Would she scream for them to stop the car? Would Lilly be happy to see her? Would she cry? There were so many scenarios playing out in her mind as they drove on in silence.

Detective Prescott eyed her from across the back seat. He leaned forward and let his chin rest in his hands as he tried to find the right words to fill the silence. He noticed Beth tense up each time they passed a mother and child on the street. When you're a detective on a case like this, there is never peace in your mind. It's like a continuous whirlwind until, in a moment, much like magic, the mind zeros in on a detail. That kind of detail can shift you in a direction. He was in the whirlwind right now, waiting for the magic to set in. Patiently, he waited for his next direction, wondering when it would come and hoping it would come soon.

They arrived shortly at Anna's condo. It was a beautiful complex, La Casa Bonita, with a Spanish design and feel. There were stunning ocean blue tiles decorating the entryway. The best feature, as far as Daniel was concerned, was the gated entry. The iron fence would give Beth some security while she was there. Also, the department assigned officers to guard the area around the clock, both uniformed and undercover. Prescott felt confident this would be the best place for Beth while they tried to solve the case and find Lilly. Now he needed to figure out how to tell Beth she wouldn't be allowed to join the search. He knew it wasn't going to go over well.

They had given Anna the assignment of questioning the witness, which she was a natural at. There wasn't a person alive that could resist her charm. Anna was fifty-four years old and retired from the Moore police department. She excelled as a police officer in her prime, but retired early due to a leg injury. She was the supervising officer at the time, and happened to be the closest to the scene of the crime when the call came out. Anna gave chase as soon as she exited her vehicle. The suspect was nearly in her grasp when he jumped a fence, and she followed. Unfortunately, she landed hard and blew out her knee as soon as her feet hit the ground. Her knee had practically turned to mush as a result of the injury, and Anna was forced to medical out once the doctors said there was nothing more they could do.

It was heart wrenching to the whole department, and especially to Anna herself. She was in no way ready to retire, or in her words, "lie down and die," so she volunteered her time. Anna was a catch all. She ran committees, filed records, and just about anything around the department she could find to busy herself. And she was irreplaceable. They regarded her as the crown jewel. Everybody it was aware of it except Anna. Daniel knew she wanted to serve any way she could. Right now, Beth would be her personal case because she had already stepped up and helped them the night Lilly went missing. It was an asset to them that Anna suffered from insomnia. Any time she couldn't sleep, she'd turn on the police scanner and listen. It was like she lived vicariously through the dispatches. Daniel knew that even before Frank called Anna that night, she'd already started brainstorming how she could help. It was just how she rolled. And when Frank mentioned he needed the manager of the Walgreen's store called, it was no surprise to them that she already knew who the manager was and had his phone number ready to hand over to them.

They entered the condo and as Anna took Beth on a tour of the home, Frank and Daniel headed toward the kitchen where the smells of rich Italian food filled the air with garlic and onion. Before they were four steps inside the house, Abel, Anna's brother, appeared, wiping his hands on a towel. Frank hugged him tightly in greeting. "That smells great! What's for dinner?" They walked toward the kitchen, leaving Daniel to wander toward the back of the condo. He peered out the back curtains. There was a patio off the living room that faced the community pool. It was about five o'clock in the evening and the sky was just beginning to take on an orange glow across the horizon, hinting nightfall would soon be upon them. Daniel stepped out onto the patio to get some fresh air.

Out on the Spanish styled patio, he could finally relax. The night's events sucked the life from him and weighed him down. He figured once they left here, which would no doubt be after dinner since Frank was so taken with Abel's waiting meal, he'd head home and try to relax with the rest of the overworked. Slumping down in a lounge chair, he folded his hands behind his head, thankful for the moment of quiet. His bed with a fluffy down comforter sounded wonderful right now.

No sooner did the thought of his bed enter his mind when his phone rang. He jumped unexpectedly. The voice on the other end of the line wasn't recognizable. He tried to force his mind to make name and voice recognition. For several seconds he failed, but then he realized it was the manager from Walgreen's speaking in an excited high pitch tone.

Daniel attempted to concentrate. He stood up and began pacing the length of the patio. "Wait, slow down and explain to me everything you just said." He threw his free hand nervously through his hair as he listened intently.

The man on the other line, who Frank had nicknamed Pajama Man, sucked in an audible breath before he spoke again. "I made a copy of the tape," he stuttered through the line. "I know you told me not to, but I have a suspect," he added quickly. "His face and name are sitting right in front of me on my computer screens."

Daniel's feet froze as if they were paralyzed by the manager's words. Finally, he was able to understand just what had the man breathing hard and talking feverishly. Anger boiled his blood that visibly rose and filled his flesh in red blotches. He swore under his breath that he would kill the guy when he saw him next. Hastily, he yanked his notepad from his breast pocket and patted his pockets, searching for his pen. "Where are you?" he demanded through gritted teeth. There was a moment of silence on the other line, and Daniel could feel his patience being tested. Finally, the caller uttered an address that Daniel hastily jotted down. "We're on our way," said Daniel, not bothering to try to hide his annoyance with the man before he hung up on him. Daniel tried to calm his nerves as he yanked the sliding door open. The words the man said were the magic Daniel was waiting for. The whirlwind delivered its first promising lead. Exhilaration shot Daniel's feet forward.

Chapter 13

Beth was slowly warming up to Anna. The lady seemed kind, like a mother. It was a good feeling to be looked after. The guest room in the condo was comfortable. It was decorated in a soft pink all over. Beth sat on the bed and silently wished to be alone so she could curl up under the covers. The pink lace calmed her. It reminded her of something, but she couldn't quite put her finger on it. She ran her hand across the bedspread, flattening its nonexistent wrinkles. It was several minutes before Anna said anything to Beth about her situation.

"How are you feeling, Beth?" Anna's thick Hispanic accent gently cut the silence between them.

Beth softly moved her hand to her swollen belly. Any time someone asked a pregnant woman how she was feeling, they silently implied how the pregnancy was going. "I feel better now, thank you." Beth didn't want to elaborate on anything yet. She wasn't sure who she could trust.

Being in the hospital brought back so many painful feelings, feelings of loss and emptiness. But now, she felt safe and welcome.

Beth could tell Anna was a kind person. It radiated from her. Compassion seemed carved into every wrinkle and every pore on her body. Beth didn't feel like she was being judged by Anna. It's strange how you can just tell when some people are good, and others make your skin crawl with apprehension.

"You must be due any day now, right?" asked Anna as she crossed her hands over her own belly.

Beth smiled and rubbed her tummy. "Yes."

"Do you know what you're having?"

Beth continued to rub her belly slowly. The question settled in her brain and she stopped as she thought about the question. She realized she couldn't answer.

"I, I didn't have a doctor, so I don't know. They did an ultrasound at the hospital," she added. Confusion twisted across her face. "I didn't think to ask. I have, I mean, I had a little girl, so I guess it would be right of me to want a little boy." She looked up at Anna and smiled. "I guess I haven't given it much thought."

There was a silence that followed her statement. She could tell Anna was a bit confused by her revelation, so she attempted to offer up an explanation.

"I mean, it's not like I haven't thought about the baby. Naturally, I have. It's just that I've been so confused lately with all that's been going on." She paused and reached for a throw pillow. "I have a feeling it isn't a boy. I guess it's just a Mommy instinct." She hugged the pillow tightly to her chest. "I wanted to go to see a doctor, but G—I mean my boyfriend — wouldn't let me. He didn't even want the baby. I didn't want to anger him, so I never asked to go. She smiled up at Anna before she continued. "It was just easier not to argue with him, you know?" Beth added cautiously. She didn't want to keep the conversation focused on the baby's father. She didn't want to talk about him.

Beth lowered her eyes back down to her belly and stroked it once more. "I was planning on leaving him before I got this far along, but I guess I was just a coward."

Anna smiled at her kindly. Beth returned the smile, but guardedly, before she bowed her head in anticipation of the waiting questions. She knew they were coming, and she completely understood, but she wasn't ready to talk, so she halted Anna's words before she could start.

"Listen, Anna. You've been so kind in letting me stay here. I do appreciate it, but the last 24 hours have been the worst of my life and I'm afraid I can't take any more." She gently closed her eyes to ward off the tears that began to pool under her lids. Hugging her bed pillow, she felt comfort from the feel of the fabric squishing under her fingers. She heard Anna sigh.

"I'm a mother myself. I have two beautiful, grown sons. I'm very lucky to have them. I haven't lost a child in the way you have, but I've lost a child." There was a great heaving moment of silence before Anna continued speaking.

"She was just a baby when she died, two months old, to be exact."

Beth felt her heart sink. She tried not to react. She sat up and listened intently.

"The doctors told me she wouldn't live very long. She had a rare disease. It was something that couldn't be treated." Anna sucked in a deep breath. "I packed up her baby girl's things after she died and stored them high in the attic. I never looked at them again. It was too painful. A huge part of me is still boxed up in the attic," she said as a far-off look covered her face.

98

"I wanted to enjoy her like she was normal when she was alive. I remember wanting to experience walking through a mall with a tiny new baby in the stroller, so I packed her up, and we went to the mall."

Beth watched Anna face relive the pain.

Anna's trembling hand fumbled with a loose strand of her hair as she tried to tuck it back behind her ear. "I put Carla in the stroller and we walked through the mall together. I was beginning to enjoy the smiles from people as they passed us, and noticed a cute, tiny baby wrapped in soft blankets. It was such an average Mommy moment. Carla was too young to enjoy it or react, but somehow, she seemed to know she was creating a memory for me."

Anna's eyes glassed over.

"We sat down at the food court and I glanced at her and I swear to you she looked like she was smiling. There was such an angelic look on her face. I leaned over and I kissed her gently on the cheek. I wanted to thank her for making my day so perfect." Anna's voice caught in her throat. "It was then that I heard a soft release of air. It was Carla's last breath escaping her lungs."

"I thought if I could get her help, maybe she'd make it. I remember screaming. I don't know if I was saying anything or just howling like a madwoman. People swarmed around us, but no one could help. She was gone." Anna wiped a tear from her cheek.

She stood and replaced the photo of her sons where it belonged on the dresser, but she didn't let go of Beth's hand.

"I hope you feel comfortable here with us. We mean to only help you. My brother Abel has cooked a wonderful meal. We would love you to join us once you're settled in here." She gave Beth's hand a gentle pat and then pulled away. As Anna turned toward the door, Beth stood and threw her arms around her.

"Thank you," was all Beth could manage.

A gentle knock came on the door and Abel stuck his head in the room.

"I'm so sorry to interrupt you two ladies, but Anna, I need to speak with you." He motioned for Anna to follow him out and then turned his attention to Beth.

"Beth, dinner is ready whenever you are. Please join us shortly."

His tone was kind and inviting. Beth couldn't help but nod her head, agreeing to the dinner invitation. Anna excused herself and joined Abel in the hall while Beth set out to freshen up. The door closed, and the weight on her heart grew heavy. She desperately hoped she wouldn't face the lifelong pain poor Anna had to face. Silently, she prayed Lilly would come home soon.

Abel and Anna stepped into the hall, but Beth could hear them talking through the thin walls. Abel spoke to Anna in a hushed whisper.

"The detectives needed to leave. They won't be joining us for dinner."

"Oh, but why? Did something happen? Frank won't be pleased. He was really looking forward to eating."

"I know, but it seems there have been some developments. Daniel got a call from the Walgreen's manager a few minutes ago. I guess the guy made an extra copy of the tape, and he's some kind of computer wizard. He said he was able to uncover a plate number. Anna, our friends flew out of this house like wind. That was all they told me. I never saw two men move so fast. I threw Frank a piece of garlic bread as he went through the front door."

Chapter 14

Ten minutes later, Beth, Anna, and Abel sat around the dinner table. At first, Beth felt uncomfortable, but the way the brother and sister interacted together helped her relax. There was a great sense of family in the way they joked and picked at one another. The love they showed was heartwarming to Beth. She envied it. Mutely, she hoped her two children would share the same closeness she was witnessing.

Abel was a fantastic cook, and his spaghetti was marvelous. Beth couldn't remember a time when she ate as heartily as she did during that meal.

The conversation was light, but soon the focus shifted to Beth. It was an easy change and Beth merged right into it without much care or notice. Anna turned to Beth after she set down her white wine. Beth was trying to sift through the events that brought her to this dinner table. The questions actually seemed to help her figure things out. She welcomed the questions now, like a child ready for show and tell.

"Beth, what made you decide to choose Oklahoma for your refuge? Or were you simply passing through to somewhere else?"

That was a great question, Beth thought as she considered it before responding. She knew the answer would confuse even the sharpest intellect. She did her best to answer. "My mother and father live here. We had a huge falling out when I was a teenager and I left. I haven't been back since." She paused as she considered her next words, because she knew they wouldn't settle well on anybody's ears. Her thoughts didn't even settle well with her.

"I don't know if I really had any intention of actually seeing my parents. I think I just wanted to pass by my old stomping ground before I moved on to where ever. It sounds confusing, I know, but I guess I wanted some kind of closure to that part of my life before I started again."

Beth could feel the inquisitive eyes of Anna and Abel as if they were trying to peer into her mind. She could feel their questions even if they didn't act on it by demanding answers, and she couldn't blame them for that.

"Would you like us to take you to your mother's? You could accomplish what you set out to do and if you wanted to call on them, we would be with you. Perhaps, it would be a good idea to stop in for a few words?" stated Abel said as he chewed on a piece of garlic bread. He cast his eyes intermittently between the two ladies at the table.

A spark grew in Anna's eyes. "We could definitely do that, if you would like. They might be able to help us find Lilly!"

Beth considered the idea for a fleeting moment, and then she tossed the idea aside. She hadn't realized until that moment that simply crossing into Oklahoma was the closure she needed. She left her childhood home long ago, and even though she couldn't recall the details of such an abrupt departure, she knew it was probably for the best never to return. She twisted her fork around the spaghetti, spinning the long strands around and around on the plate until her fork was completely surrounded. Slowly, she looked up at Anna and Abel, who waited for her response.

"Thank you, but I think I'm ready to let go and move on. All I can think of right now is finding Lilly and they don't even know she exists."

Anna looked up sharply from her meal.

"It wouldn't help to talk with them. That demon isn't one I'm ready to face."

Abel cautiously returned to his meal. Anna, on the other hand, placed her fork on the table and reached for her napkin. After she wiped her face clean, she turned her attention back to Beth.

"Do you know where your parents live?"

"Well, the address I have written down is in a town called Weshure, just northwest of here. I don't know if they still live here, or if they're even alive, but I think they're still there," replied Beth, as she set her fork down on her plate. She was absolutely stuffed and didn't think she could take another bite.

"Well Beth, if you change your mind and you want to go, Abel and I would be more than happy to take you," offered Anna as she finished off her glass of wine in a final sip.

Beth gently pushed her plate aside, confirming to herself she was finished with the meal. She placed her hand gently on the top of her belly, where her pregnancy heartburn had begun to rise. Turning her attention to Anna, she smiled. "Thank you, but I want to stay here and help with the search for Lilly."

Chapter 15

The detectives pulled up at the tiny brick house on Huddleston Drive. The neighborhood was quiet except for the sound of a dog barking in the distance. The sky was just beginning to turn a perfect shade of ocean blue. It wasn't quite dark, but hinting that night would soon overcome them. The house was quiet.

Daniel was fired up. Frank, on the other hand was calm and collected. He'd been lecturing Daniel the entire time about how, despite the fact that the Walgreen's manager was interfering with their investigation and tampering with evidence, he'd done exactly what either one of them would have done in the same situation. He thought the guy should get a medal for his boldness. It was very commendable.

Daniel threw the car into park, the anger boiled inside him like hot lava. He turned and locked eyes on Frank. "You might want to go in first, because I'm livid right now!" Daniel plucked the keys from the ignition.

Frank didn't respond. He just reached for the handle and exited the car. Anything he said would be met with an argument from his partner. All he could do was let him simmer for a bit. He hoped Ben Williams, formerly known as Pajama Man, produced something solid, so his partner would have more cause to refrain from killing the guy. He could only hope because he was fond of the guy.

They walked in unison to the front door of the L- shaped house. It was a typical Oklahoma home. The red brick revealed a huge crack, no doubt caused by weathering many fierce storms. Frank would guess it was built in the 60s because of the style. Slowly he pushed the doorbell and anticipated the war that was about to erupt between the Pajama Man and Daniel. He held his breath as the wooden door swung open.

No sooner did the door swing open than Frank felt himself abruptly pushed aside by Daniel. Frank followed the big bad wolf into the house. With a brisk turn, he shut the door.

By the look on his face, he didn't know what hit him. Daniel held his elbow firmly under Ben's throat as he glared into the man's eyes.

Frank stood back. He would intervene, but not until he knew it was necessary. He needed to make sure the control stayed with

Daniel. Frank knew Daniel was just trying to piss on his property, claiming it as his own once again. Frank couldn't blame him. What the Walgreen's manager did for them was honorable. It wasn't right, but it was honorable, and he knew his partner appreciated it deep down inside.

They'd been partners long enough for Frank to know Daniel only wanted to make a point, that they were actually the ones in charge of the investigation and they'd be the ones calling all the shots. It was a necessary evil in police work. Someone needed to be the bad cop, and someone had to be the good cop. It was just the way it worked. You could switch it up whenever necessary, but there could never be two in the same role. It was an unspoken rule and a technique that worked like a charm every time.

Frank took a quick look around. The avocado green kitchen off to the right, ugly wood paneling along some of the walls, and a popcorn ceiling revealed the house was definitely stuck in the sixties. It was small, dull and undecorated, but a familiar hum suddenly reached his ears and perked his interest.

The swearing from his partner stopped him from exploring the house further. "All right! Frank yelled as he placed himself between Ben and his partner. "Knock it off. Let's see what this guy has to show us," he ordered as he tried to control the situation. "Come on Pajama Man; let's see what you've got."

"You can call me Ben."

"Huh?"

"Ben, it's my name. Not Pajama Man."

"Oh right, well, whatever your name is, let's go." He roughly pushed the two of them apart and stepped back himself. He watched as his partner eased up on the guy and turned toward Daniel.

Frank walked towards the humming as he searched for a light. He found one against a wall that displayed an entertainment center with a gentle glow of a television illuminating from it. Gently, he flicked on the switch that revealed a surprising sight.

He squinted as his eyes slowly adjusted. There in front of him was a room filled wall to wall with computers. Each one was glowing and pulsing with electronic life. Frank eyed his partner, who was slowly returning to himself. His green hulk's anger was diminishing right before Frank's eyes.

"What the hell?"

The living room faced the back of the house. It was small, but it contained six huge computers. A couch and coffee table sat in the center of the room, but the rest was filled with electronics. It was fascinating. The two detectives stared, dumbfounded. *What was this guy's real story?*

In that moment, a jet from the nearby Air Force base flew over the home, waking them all from the trance they'd slipped into. It only took a few seconds to pass the house, but in those seconds, a million questions formed in Frank's mind.

Pajama Man seemed to sense their apprehension and stepped forward.

"I mentioned I was a computer geek. Well, it's more of a passion I guess," he cleared his throat. "I went to school, but I never had the courage to actually do something with the degree." He readjusted his glasses and gave a crooked smile.

"I took the tape because I wanted to help," he explained. "I thought maybe if I could get a plate number, that maybe I could help save the girl. I'm sorry," he added flatly as he adjusted his glasses again and hung his head.

Daniel stopped short at one of the computer screens. It took him several moments to dissect the image displayed on it. His own police crew hadn't, as of yet, discovered what was flashing on the screen. It was a name.

"George Smith, what does that mean?" asked Daniel as he turned toward the man he had just moments before pinned against the wall.

The detectives stared at Ben Williams with mirrored, confused expressions as they waited for him to reply. Ben looked at them cautiously.

"That's the name of the owner of the van. I was able to figure it out with 99.9% certainty."

A grin spread across Frank's face as his respect for Pajama Man grew. He watched Ben pride fully as a sly smile crept across the man's face.

Chapter 16

Daniel couldn't contain himself. His excitement bubbled over as a smirk filled his face. He slapped his hand down enthusiastically across Ben's back, jolting him forward. Daniel felt confident in what Ben had uncovered. It was their next lead. The familiar whirlwind sensation spun around him. He always knew when a lead was strong. It was like a force of nature was filling him from within. His blood ran smoothly and his energy was soaring. He didn't know how the guy pulled it off, but he was thankful he hadn't just killed him right there on the entryway floor.

The other computers contained details of their suspect's life. He was from Arkansas, like they suspected, and he was a dirtbag. His rap sheet was over ten pages long. He'd committed crimes of assault, robbery, drug dealing and a list of DUIs. He'd served time a few years back. Daniel was looking forward to catching the guy and bringing him in for his final and most permanent arrest.

They consumed all the information presented and left the house quicker than they'd come. Determination pushed their feet to the car and on the path toward justice. The burden they carried all day suddenly depleted and faith filled the void.

Daniel made a call to their chief and informed him of what they discovered and where they were headed. The chief said he'd call Anna and have her make arrangements for their departing flight out of Oklahoma. Anticipation filled the car ride to the airport. While Daniel drove, Frank read the pages of information recovered from Ben's house aloud. They wanted to be familiar with every detail of their suspect's life. The information would have an effect on the technique they'd used to interrogate him.

Once they got to the airport, they were expedited through security. They were required to declare their side arms upon check in. It was standard procedure, but an annoying one. They were relieved to find that Anna had arranged for them to fly first class. The foot room would make it possible for them to get some much-needed sleep.

The flight to Arkansas was too quick for much sleep, but it didn't matter. They realized they were too wired, anyway. They wanted to be there when the asshole George was arrested. Upon landing, a uniformed officer from the Arkansas State Police greeted them. He informed them George Smith had been found passed out in his trailer. They took him into custody for questioning. The guy was too drunk to object to the intrusion.

The town of Dyer didn't have a police force, but they were detaining the suspect in a public town building until the detectives could get there to interview him. Then they'd decide what needed to be done with him. If he was to be arrested, he'd be transferred to Fort Smith and remain in custody with the Arkansas State Police department until instructed otherwise by the FBI.

The officer also informed the detectives that Lilly hadn't been found in George's custody. So far, no evidence indicated she was ever in his care. That didn't sit well with Daniel. He was beginning to fear the worst. He hoped the little girl would have been found by now, but the fact that she hadn't didn't mean the suspect didn't know where she was. His van was at the scene of the crime and there was little doubt the guy knew where she was being kept. Daniel just had to get the guy to talk.

The drive to Dyer was agonizing. Every road and small community they passed appeared abandoned. Daniel couldn't imagine how anyone could live out in such an isolated area. The fields surrounding the roads were overgrown and pitiful. The region was lost and desolate. It looked like time had deserted it, forgetting it even existed. It probably had. Based on the research he did on the plane; Dyer had a population somewhere around eight hundred. It was tiny in comparison to Moore, Oklahoma.

They pulled into the Dyer Town Hall with a great sense of urgency. They received word that their suspect wasn't cooperating with the police. He wasn't asking for a lawyer either, which was good. Daniel wanted just five minutes with the guy. There was a long list of questions, but he planned on starting with the most important question, hoping to skip the small talk.

They were escorted inside the building. It appeared as abandoned as the town itself. There was dust swimming around in the air and it smelled of rot and dirt. Daniel felt certain it remained unoccupied most of the time, and perhaps excitement like this was the only time this building saw any action. He doubted days like this came very often.

Once inside, Daniel scanned the room. Nothing was organized. There was a desk in the left corner, covered with papers and surrounded by stacks of boxes. There were loose papers stacked freely on the floor. They walked toward the back of the building where a uniformed officer waited, guarding a closed door.

Stepping aside, the officer let the detectives enter first. The room was dark with the exception of a green desk side lamp illuminating the room with great strain. The curtains were pulled closed, and a man sat in a chair with his right handcuffed to a pole that stuck out from the wall. A small table was placed in front of him and a single chair waited on the other side of the table.

Frank stepped back as Daniel approached the man who reeked of whiskey mixed with body odor. His hair was disheveled and greasy. It looked like it hadn't been washed in months. He appeared to be in his mid-to late twenties, but he was aging quickly due to his rough life style. The man was wearing a dirty gray sweater and faded black jeans. He was thin and gaunt looking. Daniel pulled out his seat and sat down across from him. He clasped his hands and set them on the table in front of the suspect as he eyed the man sitting before him. He noticed the man's face was so filthy that dirt was caked in the creases of his skin.

Daniel didn't speak for several seconds. The man grinned and threw a cocky smile, but within several seconds discomfort spread across his face. He was chewing on a toothpick nervously. Daniel eased forward, locked eyes with the suspect, and yanked the toothpick from his lips. The game was on.

"So, where's Lilly?" He leaned forward to an inch from the dirt covered face, closing the gap between them. There was no response from the man across from him. "Let me rephrase the question. Where is Lilly?" he restated firmly through pursed lips, his patience growing thin. He wasn't in the mood for games. Taking a look at his watch, he made a mental note of how many days it had been since the girl was taken.

This time, the man looked up at him. His cocky attitude was slowly returning. "What the fuck are you talking about?"

Daniel didn't flinch as the words splatted his face. He expected sarcasm from the scumbag. Dealing with men like this was routine for him.

Feeling unmoved by the criminal's nasty attitude, Daniel reworded his question. This time, he let his distaste show even more. "I want to know where the little girl is that you took two nights ago. You know, the one who belongs to the pregnant woman you tried to kill."

Laughter escaped from the suspect. He was laughing so hard a coughing fit overcame him. Finally, he caught his breath and grinned at Prescott. His teeth presented their yellow, decaying layers of filth.

"You think I took a little girl and beat up a pregnant woman? Shit, you're one stupid mother fucker. I didn't touch no woman, and I didn't take no girl," he spat.

Just then, the suspect was smacked in the back of the head by Frank. The suspect threw him a dirty look as he rubbed the back of his head with his free hand.

"All right, let me catch you up to speed then," Daniel said, crossing his arms in front of him. "Two nights ago, your van was caught on camera in Moore, Oklahoma, where a little girl turned up missing. You were seen on tape, putting something in the back of your van." He returned a mirrored cocky smile as he relayed what they knew.

"Now, you can sit there and lie to me and we can make this very painful, or you can admit what we already know and tell us where the girl is. That is as simple as it's going to get for you." Daniel inched closer again. He could tell the guy was getting

119

nervous because beads of sweat were beginning to pop up on his forehead. He bit his bottom lip as his knee jiggled slightly.

"I didn't take no girl," he spat out the words like they tasted bitter on his tongue.

Daniel leaned back off the table and crossed his arms once again. He decided a different approach might be better.

"All right, then tell me what you did take."

The man stopped squirming and ran his free hand through his hair. "All right, I'll tell you what happened, but we didn't take no little girl."

Daniel sat back in his seat and folded his arms stiffly across his chest. He locked his eyes on the man in front of him as he prepared to hear what he had to say.

"My van was in Oklahoma two nights ago. That much is true, but I swear to you, I didn't take no little girl."

"Start from the beginning." He wanted the suspect to take the lead. It was a technique that was used to help the suspect feel like they still had some control, even if they had none.

"I was out driving one night and I saw James running down the road. He looked like he'd just been beaten up. I stopped to tease him a little. I thought maybe he had pissed someone off. He has a reputation for doing that," George explained. "He told me I had to give him a ride. I tried to refuse, but he told me some bitch took off with his guitar and if I'd give him a ride, he'd pay me." The man raked his free hand through his hair again.

Daniel eyed Frank cautiously. If what this dirt bag was saying was true, then they had the wrong guy. Daniel knew he needed to start asking questions in order to speed up the investigation.

With mocking words, Daniel pressed his suspect. "So, you drove this James guy to Moore, Oklahoma?" His eyes shifted between the suspect and his partner. He didn't know if he believed the guy yet. "You need to tell me more, and tell me quick, because what you've said so far isn't making much sense and my partner over there is feeling ready to cuff your sorry ass right now."

George hesitated as he looked around the room, but his eyes shifted downward as he appeared to give up the fight to refrain from talking.

"Yes. He said his bitch beat him up and stole his guitar and he needed to get it back. He said it was very important to him. We didn't know we were going to Oklahoma when we started driving. We just started driving," he stated defensively. He held his head on his elbow and again ran his hand through his greasy hair.

"Then we needed gas, so we stopped at the Quick Gas down the street. James went inside while I pumped and when he came out, he was cursing up a storm and excited about something." He threw his hand down on the table nervously and played with his cup of water. "James ordered me to start driving again. I didn't know why he was so excited until we were on our way. He ordered me to get on the interstate." George's knees began the same nervous shake from earlier, picking up speed as he continued the story. Daniel couldn't tell if the guy was just nervous or having some kind of withdrawal from drugs. He suspected the guy was freaking out about something though, something he hadn't shared with the detectives yet, and it was only a matter of time before Daniel got it out of him.

"I guess his girlfriend Irene, from the Quick Gas, said she'd seen his other girlfriend Beth buying maps for Oklahoma not too long before we got there. So, that's where he wanted to go. He wanted to get on the 40 and we just drove on and on, hoping to find her," he added. "I thought it was stupid. James is a loose cannon

122

kind of guy, though. He was so bloody and messed up, I didn't want to argue with him, and so I just drove."

Daniel tried to understand what he'd learned. "I don't get it. How did you catch up to her? If she had a head start and you had little idea where she was going, how did you find her?" He was silently hoping that the suspect wouldn't be able to answer that question. Then he'd know it was all a lie.

George gave a grin as he turned his eyes slowly up to the detective. "Well, that's the funny part. We were about to give up when we pulled over along the side of the highway and just sat there for a while. James was trying to decide what to do and then he got all excited again when he saw his Chevy Malibu pass us. He said it had to be her because the car is avocado green with a maroon-colored quarter panel. Well, sure as shit, that same kind of car just passed us, so we started driving again and we followed the car."

At this point, Daniel was pacing the room. "So, you followed her to Moore, Oklahoma, and then took the little girl?"

"Shit, dudes, aren't you listening? We didn't take no little girl!" the suspect shouted. His irritation spilled over like lava. He pressed his lips together and spat out the toothpick he'd been holding and chewing the entire time.

Daniel lunged forward; his face nearly pressed against the suspect's. "Then why the hell are you so nervous?" His anger exploded across the room. "You're sitting there telling me you didn't take a little girl, but you're nervous like a whore on Melrose, so you took something, or maybe you did something that you don't want us to figure out, but I have news for you, you will be going to jail for kidnapping, because a little girl is exactly what was taken that day, and unless you can tell me something different, there's nothing I can do for you." Prescott locked his eyes hard on his suspect as he drove his next words home. "The FBI will be here any minute and they'll take you into custody, unless you can explain how you went there to get something back and a little girl is gone!"

The suspect cringed and trembled under the detective's stare. His eyes lost focus and his determination waned. Daniel could tell he was about to crumble. He'd seen it dozens of times, and sure enough, the man caved.

"He didn't tell me what we were taking. He went up to her car, smashed the window and took a guitar case from the front seat.

It was the guitar case he hid his money in. That was it, though. He didn't take anything else," he added before tears spilled from his eyes. His tough-guy image crumbled into pieces.

Daniel cringed. His stomach bloated with bile that wanted to escape. He believed the guy. None of it made sense, but he believed the guy.

"This guy, James, what's his last name and where does he live?"

The suspect buckled in his chair, and his face plummeted into his hands.

Daniel stood up as he sensed the suspect's next words would be disturbing. His feet carried him restlessly back and forth across the floor.

"His name is James Blake, and he lives in a trailer off of Curtis Street. But you aren't going to find him," he said.

"What do you mean, we aren't going to find him?" A warning shot across his flesh. Somewhere in his gut, he knew what George was going to say.

"You aren't going to find him because he's dead."

Daniel watched as the man's eyes seemed to turn to ice and a dark emptiness filled them.

Chapter 17

Beth woke early. She found a book in her room, so she sat and thumbed through it. She wanted to read it to escape, but her mind couldn't focus. Rubbing a hand over her abdomen, she let her thoughts wander to the baby within. It wouldn't be long before the baby would be here. The thought gave her strength to face the day. She slowly rose from her bed, her swollen feet gliding over the wooden floor as she moved toward the bedroom window.

Her room overlooked the community pool. It looked inviting, and the thought of sitting by the water sounded fantastic. She hadn't been able to enjoy any kind of relaxing activities lately and wanted to feel the sun kiss her skin. The bedroom door gave a tiny squeak as it opened. If anyone was still asleep, she didn't want to wake them. Slowly, she crept down the steps toward the back sliding door. Everyone was still asleep. Snoring came from Abel's room.

She clicked the lock on the sliding door and slipped outside. The cool morning air awakened her senses. Once she crossed into the pool area, she quietly pulled up a lounge chair. She sank clumsily down into it, doubting that getting out would be easy. The sun was waking up and she could tell it was going to be another hot, humid day, but right now it felt absolutely perfect. A blissful sense of comfort enveloped her. Before long, her eyes grew heavy and sleep crept up on her.

A dream clouded her mind. In her dream, there was a house. It was an old, two-story farmhouse with a tall windmill spinning in the yard. The yard surrounding the house seemed to go on forever, and tall, golden grass blew gently in the breeze. There was something very familiar about the residence, but Beth couldn't quite figure out what it was. A large wrap-around porch encased the dwelling from front to back. She was about to climb the beaten steps and enter the house to check it out when she heard crying coming from somewhere. Beth stopped short and listened.

The crying ceased, but she took a guess at the direction it came from. She began walking toward the left side of the house, listening with intent as she walked. Once she rounded the corner, she noticed a storm shelter. Leaning down, she listened closer. It was then that she heard the crying from below. It was child's muffled cry. Her hands shook as she reached for the door. She was terrified to open it, but she knew she needed to find out what was beyond those wooden doors.

Beth heard the cry once more. She thought it sounded familiar. It sounded like Lilly. Terror gripped her heart as she fumbled with the latch. It was locked. Beth panicked, and she looked around for something to smash the lock. Off to the side of the shelter, she found a large rock. She was afraid to make too much noise, so she took off her sweater and wrapped the boulder in it, hoping it would muffle the sound. Once she was ready, she slammed it with all the strength she had until the lock broke. Relief filled her heart when she realized the lock was broken, and pure determination inched her forward.

She flung the doors opened. Dust flew up in her face, causing her to cough and gag. She fanned the dry, dirt filled air and took the first step down into the darkness below, hoping her feet would land on a solid step. Each step down made it harder and harder to see. The whimpering grew louder the closer she got.

She followed the sound, blind and terrified. Her hands searched the darkness for something, anything, and nothing all at the same time. She crouched lower and lower towards the floor where the crying seemed to be coming from. Before long, she was crawling forward on her hands and knees on the cold, dirty ground. Finally, her hands found something.

A small window allowed the sun to creep into her eyes. Slowly, they began to adjust. A silhouette emerged from within the darkness. She could tell she was touching a small child. The youngster had a head full of long, curly hair. Beth knew then that the child was a little girl. She was crying in a soft, low mumble. Beth couldn't tell if it was Lilly or not at that point. Suddenly, she heard a noise coming from the floor above them. She desperately wanted to quiet the little girl.

"Shhhh. It's okay. You're okay now. I'm going to get you out of here, but you have to stop crying or they will find us. Okay?" She patted the little girl, but she didn't seem to notice. The child continued to cry and whimper. It was then that Beth noticed the clothes the girl was wearing. They were the same clothes Lilly was wearing the day she was taken. The little ladybug outfit was filthy now. Beth reached for the girl and turned her face so she could see her in the light. Lilly! Beth found her daughter! She scooped Lilly up in her arms and turned toward the way she'd come, determined they would leave the wretched place together.

She carried Lilly, shushing her the entire way. The sun lit the opening to the shelter at the top of the stairs so it was easy to find, but Lilly was heavy and the hallway seemed to go on forever. Lilly's crying grew louder, and Beth now heard voices from above. She needed to get out before whoever it was overhead discovered them trying to escape. She lunged for the steps, taking them two at a time, but before she could get to the top, the doors above them slammed shut with a sickening thud, trapping them inside. Beth panicked and screamed. She reached for the doors and banged on them, but they wouldn't budge. She cried and yelled as she realized she was now a prisoner along with Lilly.

Beth glanced down and realized at that moment her arms were empty. Lilly was gone. She turned and searched the darkness, but she was nowhere to be found. She called for Lilly, but there was no response. No crying. No words. Only silence.

Beth searched the darkness for several minutes. She fumbled clumsily through the room, searching for anything to give her a hint of where they were and who she was dealing with. Before long, she found a light dangling from above. She pulled on the string and the room illuminated with a soft, dull glow. Beth scrambled to search the room for Lilly, but she found it completely empty. The only things the room contained were boxes and crates. She was the only occupant of this musty prison.

***

The terror of the dream jolted Beth awake. She found herself dripping in sweat, laying in the lounge chair. She doubted much time had passed since she'd fallen asleep. The memory of what she dreamt scorched her, filling her will grief. It felt so real. Anguish swallowed her and the tears cascaded down her cheeks, taking part of her soul with them. Her hands layered her face in a shielding mask and she wept.

She didn't know how long she cried by the pool, but suddenly she felt like her gut was being ripped apart. The pain was unbearable. It sliced through her back and wrapped all the way around to her belly. It felt like her abdomen was going to implode. Beth grabbed for her stomach. After a few seconds of agony, the pain subsided and Beth could breathe again. She raised herself to a sitting position as she analyzed what had happened.

The only thing it could have been was a contraction. She tried to think of what contractions felt like when she had Lilly, but she couldn't remember. She gazed across the lawn towards the condo she left a while ago. It seemed so distant. She decided she'd wait a little bit, hoping someone would come looking for her, and then another wrenching pain gripped her. It clawed at her. As soon as she thought the pain was gone, she was filled with a tremendous sense of fear. Moisture dribbled between her legs. It didn't feel like her water broke, so between her sobs, she pulled up her nightgown.

When she pulled her shaking hand back so she could see, she was startled! Her fingers were coated with blood. NO! No, no, no. She was about to have her baby. Something was wrong. She couldn't focus on what to do. Help! I have to get help.

Beth didn't care anymore if she woke the entire complex. She stood and headed toward the condo. Another stabbing contraction hit her. She tried to scream, but no sound escaped. She doubled over, clutching her stomach as the pain intensified and drove her to the ground in the fetal position. Within a few seconds, the pain subsided, once again leaving her gasping for breath. Beth took her chance. She positioned her legs to stand, but they were like rubber. There was no strength left. She fell back once again and decided her only way to get help would be to crawl.

Each creep ahead on the course, sandpaper ground produced raw abrasions on her knees. Tiny pieces of rock pressed into her sore flesh as she inched into the open, but she forced herself to suffer through. She tried to yell for help once more. This time she was able to scream, but she doubted it was loud enough to wake anyone. The blood that was releasing between her legs was beginning to show through her gown. The sight of the horrible red stain was grotesque and terrifying at the same time.

She forced her body forward and was just about to reach the grass when another contraction took over her body. This time, her water did break. It gushed out of her like a flood, and her abdomen shrank right before her eyes as the fluid emptied itself from within. Beth grabbed her belly where her waiting baby lay under the skin. She needed to get help. She couldn't let something bad happen to her unborn child. Once the contraction ended, she vowed she'd scream for help with every bit of strength she had left in her.

She could feel the pain ease up and she took a deep breath and screamed louder than she'd ever screamed in her life. Her head shook from the vibrations that came from her throat. She ended the scream in a coughing fit. With each cough, she could feel wetness squish out of her. Then, sweet glory emerged from the condos around her, one after another. She saw Abel first, and Anna followed with determined steps behind. Time seemed to slow and Beth crumbled in relief onto the prickly lawn below her. The muffled cries of Anna could be heard as she urged someone to call 911.

In a blur, Beth could see Abel and Anna. She wanted to fall into the emptiness that was beckoning her, but she forced her eyes opened, searching the swirling images above her. Anna was giving Abel and the other neighbor instructions. Then she heard fear within Anna's sweet voice.

"Abel, there's a lot of blood. We need to get her to the hospital fast."

Beth could feel Anna pulling on something down below, and she wondered if her baby had been born or not. She didn't hear any crying, but she felt empty.

It was then that Beth felt her body lifted off of the grass. Abel wasn't going to wait for the ambulance to find them. He was carrying Beth to meet the sirens that screamed through the air. From the distance Beth heard someone say, "I think the baby is dead." The words lashed at her senses like hot daggers.

She closed her eyes and gave into the raging force of darkness pulling her. She would allow herself to die too, welcoming death with open arms.

Chapter 18

It didn't take long for the detectives to get confirmation of James

Blake's death. It happened just the night before, and the town was

beginning to talk. Rumors spread fast in small towns and even if

George didn't rat himself out, the detectives would have heard about

the death of James.

He lived well off the road, far out of sight of anyone, but

when his trailer exploded into flames, there was no escaping the eyes

of neighbors. A small group of people saw the smoke not long after

they heard the explosion. There didn't seem to be anyone who was

missing him or crying in the wake of the crime, except maybe his

"other" girlfriend Irene, who spent the entire night telling neighbors

how much she loved him and how she'd planned to marry him

someday.

The detectives received the details of the event from the local

police officers. That's what they called themselves anyway, even

though they were only preliminary officers. The truth was Fort

Smith, a thirty-minute drive away, handled anything bigger than a

traffic ticket. Based on what the onlookers were saying, this was the biggest event to happen in the town for a long time. No one could recall a crime that could compare. There appeared to be a silent celebration of sorts going on.

From what they were told, James was the biggest sleaze ball in town. He was far worse than their previous suspect, George. James was known for dealing in drugs. No one could prove it, though. He spent his time living isolated on his land and rumor had it that he'd go to Fort Smith to do "business." It was smart to do it that way. He could keep a low profile in town and deal heavily in a city where he didn't reside. That was how he went relatively unnoticed most of the time.

Everyone in town thought he'd end up dead by the hands of other thugs, but instead, it was greedy George who took him down. How ironic, Daniel thought as he thumbed through his brief case uncovering the image of Lilly. He kept her picture close to him all the time so he could stay focused and motivated.

George spoke the truth. He picked up James on the side of the road, and drove him to Moore, Oklahoma, where a guitar case was eventually recovered. When they got back from Moore, George asked James for payment as promised and when James refused, an argument ensued. There was a lengthy struggle. George shot him with the same rifle Beth used on him earlier. He tried covering up the crime by torching the place and making it look like an accident.

He almost got away with it too, but Daniel and Frank arrived the very next day, uncovering his deceit. The entire town was ready to sweep James' death under the rug. It was one less criminal in their world, and they were glad he was gone. George had told them going to jail for murder would be better than going to jail for kidnapping, a crime he insisted he was no part of.

Daniel was amazed by the turn of events. He felt like he was walking in a slow-motion nightmare. In only a few hours, they'd lost a suspect, a lead, and any hope of finding Lilly. He had no idea where to turn. The trailer where Beth and Lilly had lived was a crumbled pile of ashes. Nothing remained. There would be no evidence to follow and no suspect to question. The only thing left standing was a swing set in the yard untouched, yet swinging in the breeze like a ghost.

Daniel and Frank set out shortly after leaving the residence to question neighbors about Beth and Lilly, but no one knew them. They saw Beth on occasion, but they never talked to her because

139

they feared James. They had little curiosity about the family who lived off the beaten path.

The residence was far off the road and seemed to be out of sight of prying neighbors. The reason was quite obvious, due to James and his lucrative business interactions in the drug world. Therefore, the detectives once again hit that ever-insulting brick wall.

Daniel threw himself down on his hotel bed and listened to his partner snore. He was envious of the guy could drop off like that. Frank could sleep anywhere and anytime, but not Daniel. He couldn't seem to shut his mind off. The day had been long, intense, and surprising, to say the least. He felt a huge sense of disappointment crush him as he realized they were at a standstill in the investigation. He felt like someone was kicking him in the gut over and over with steel-toed boots.

They'd spent the entire day combing the area, going door to door and walking through the surrounding land. There was no trace of Lilly. *Were these people blind? They almost seemed like zombies wandering through life, never seeing, never hearing anything.* The FBI had spread out among the town, performing their own search.

The news and media swarmed in as well, filling up every corner they could with news vans and cameras. It was like the circus had come to town and Daniel was exhausted.

He kept rolling over everything he knew so far. The news and the department weren't revealing anything he didn't already know, and he was growing more downcast with each passing moment. His phone had no signal, so he was cut off from the rest of the world, with the exception of the one television station that came in on the screen. He knew sleep would be the only way to rejuvenate his broken mind, so he threw back the covers and slid between the sheets.

He battled the war in his mind for what seemed hours before sleep finally claimed him.

***

The nagging sound of the motel room phone jarred Daniel from his slumber. Feeling disoriented, he tried to figure out what the piercing noise was. He fumbled around in the location the clamor was coming from and knocked the alarm clock to the floor in the process. The sound of the shower running reminded him of where he was and he lunged for the blaring phone. He knew it had to be someone important on the other line, and he had no idea how many times it had already rung.

The dryness in his throat was refusing his voice passage. "Hello," he rasped. He instantly recognized Anna's voice on the other end. She was explaining how she'd been trying to get a hold of them for quite some time.

"We don't have cell service out here," he explained as she demanded to know why they hadn't answered their phones. He squeezed his fingertips over his eyes, trying to force the sleep from them. Anna sounded concerned, and he wanted to be able to focus on what she was saying. His pulse raced as he listened in silence.

"What! Are you serious? Do we need to come back?" He threw the questions from his mouth one after another. Feeling tired was no longer a problem. He flew to his feet and grabbed his crumbled jeans from the floor. He wedged the receiver against his ear and shoulder as he pulled on his jeans. The cord to the phone kept him pinned to the bedside, so he was only able to slide one leg into his jeans before he was forced to stop. As he listened to Anna, his heart grew heavier with each word. Thanking her, he set the phone back on the receiver.

It wasn't long before the two detectives were dressed and ready to step out into the world. Daniel relayed everything he knew to Frank as he dressed. Frank listened to every word as he gathered his belongings, his faced swaying from one emotion to the next. The story Daniel shared had stunned him into silence.

Beth developed a rare and devastating condition called placenta accrete. She showed no signs of a problem until her contractions began, which made it impossible to fix. Anna said Beth nearly died in the delivery and because she didn't deliver in a hospital when the placenta detached, it tore her insides, causing massive bleeding. In the end, they had to perform a hysterectomy. It was the only way to save Beth's life and stop the bleeding.

Anna also said Beth was so brutally drained in the delivery that she had yet to reopen her eyes and she delivered nearly twenty-four hours earlier. Daniel was worried that she wouldn't recover, and they'd already lost one key suspect in the trailer fire. If Beth died, then they might never know where to go for their next lead.

There were only two pieces of good news to come through the phone that morning. Anna reported with great pride that the baby, a girl, was alive and doing well despite her explosive entry into the world. And they may have their next lead. Anna discovered some information that she believed would help them. Daniel decided going back to Oklahoma was all they could do at this point. They had Anna get them an evening flight so they could tie up any loose ends before they left. They headed out bright and early, and despite the crisp, fresh day that embraced them, neither one felt revived. They carried the heavy burden in silence. A new set of fears clouded the horizon.

Chapter 19

Dr. Stevens watched Beth go in and out of consciousness for hours. She'd lost a tremendous amount of blood. If she'd gone into labor at a hospital, he might have been able to prevent it. The poor woman had been through so much in the past week, so he let her rest peacefully. She certainly earned that courtesy.

The baby was healthy and doing well in the nursery. The entire nursery staff was doting on the tiny girl. She'd become a sort of celebrity of the labor and delivery wing. Stevens and a colleague were assigned to only Beth and her baby's care for the time being, considering the attention the abduction was bringing to the hospital. The big guys calling the shots on the top floors didn't want anything to compromise the health of their new stars.

Dr. Stevens used his free time to research everything he could about Beth and the possible compromises that could surround her well-being. He sat within the darkness of her hospital room, where only the soft glow of his laptop computer could be seen and the gentle buzz of her monitor could be heard. He'd been investigating since she first came into his care, and he felt certain he was getting close to a conclusion of sorts. He'd never felt more baffled by any patient. The petite woman who lay unconscious was definitely giving him a run for his money.

He filled his coffee cup to the brim to help him ride the night to its completion. There was no way he was going to let anything more happen to her. Moments after he'd settled in his chair, he noticed Beth begin to stir. He watched as her gentle movements grew more fitful. He'd seen her do this several times since she delivered. Most of the time she'd settle down on her own, but other times she'd wake in a screaming fit and he'd have to rush to her side to comfort her. He wasn't quite sure what this wakeful moment would bring.

Removing his glasses, he set them down next to his computer and rose to his feet, never taking his eyes off his patient. He'd only taken a few steps when he noticed her eyes were fluttering open. Beth began to search the room for something familiar. Her lashes fluttered as her eyes tried to adjust. Suddenly, her weak eyes landed on Dr. Stevens. He leaned over, hoping she could focus better on him if he hovered closely. He noticed her try to lock her eyes onto his, but then she forced them shut as if the pain of committing her gaze was too much to handle. He tried to explain to her who he was, but she kept muttering nonsense. Leaning in closer, he tried to decode her inaudible words. In the slurred gibberish, all he could manage to make out was what he thought to be a name.

Dr. Stevens couldn't quite understand what she meant because she was completely incoherent at the time and muttering what appeared to be nonsense, but seemed to think Stevens was somebody else. She kept calling him Dr. Owens. He tried several times to ask her what she meant, but she soon fell back into unconsciousness.

After several moments of waiting to see if her eyes would open again, Dr. Stevens decided Beth wasn't going to resurface and face him. He double checked all her monitors before he walked back to his waiting laptop and a familiar sense of disappointment came over him. He couldn't help but hope next time she'd be more alert. The waiting game was growing tiresome.

He couldn't help wonder who this Dr. Owens was and why Beth was saying the name over and over with such urgency, so he researched the name. His Google search showed dozens of possible matches. One was a heart doctor in New York. Another was a dermatologist in California, but the most compelling was a psychologist in Oklahoma. Stevens decided he'd contact all the doctors on the list and see if any of them had ever had Beth Waters for a patient. His gut told him that something was off and he had to get his hands on any medical records related to her, if possible.

He tried to reason with his conscience, but he couldn't just shrug it all off. There was a pull toward the Dr. Owens in Oklahoma. The location couldn't just be a coincidence. He etched the doctor's contact information on a piece of paper, marking it as his number one priority.

He didn't know where to turn at this point, but he knew if he wanted to help his patient, then he needed to take a chance and call the guy to simply rule out the connection. It was too late in the evening to reach this Dr. Owens at his office, but he wanted the doctor to know someone was trying to get a hold of him, so he decided he'd call anyway and leave a message. Calls were placed to the other dozen doctors as well, reaching the same familiar recording system. After he left the messages, all he could do was wait for his patient to wake from her darkness and embrace the world that waited expectantly for her return.

Chapter 20

The detectives landed in Oklahoma City early that evening and recovered their car from the airport parking garage. It was exhausting to go back and forth between the extreme high of hope to a suffocating low of defeat. This case was a roller coaster, heaving them in all directions.

Daniel suggested they both go home and rest. It wasn't for his need, but rather the necessity for his partner to maintain his marriage. He didn't want Frank to deal with the wrath of his wife for being away for such a long time. Daniel watched as Frank pulled out his phone and speed dialed his wife's cell. He drove mutely while Frank spoke to his wife lovingly.

"Hey, baby. We're back in town, but we have some more things to do, so I won't be coming home tonight," explained Frank.

Daniel tried not to listen to their conversation, but it was hard not to. He admired the affection they shared for one another. He let his thoughts drift while Frank asked about the kids and what his family was up to while he was gone. It wasn't until Frank's words shifted back to the case that his ears perked up again.

"No, baby, we haven't found her. You will be one of the first to know when we do. Make sure you kiss the kids for me, okay?" said Frank before he blew a kiss into the phone and hung up.

Daniel couldn't help but smile and dart teasing glances at his partner, who in turn punched him in the arm.

"She said not to come home until we find the girl," announced Frank with a prideful smile. Frank's wife, Isabel, was quite a firecracker when it came to the children. He had little cause to think she'd ever want to put her own needs above the missing little girl. After a quick stop at McDonald's for burgers and coffee, they were back on the road. They drove on in silence for the start of the trip. The discussion of how they came across the new information came up. It was pure brilliance and bravery that led Anna to search for the information.

Anna related to Daniel that she woke the morning after the detectives left Beth at her house to find Beth lounging by the pool. She took the opportunity to go through Beth's belongings for something that would help find Lilly. She didn't expect to find much, but what she'd set out to find was the address of Beth's parents. Beth mentioned the detail very casually, but Anna had a trained ear and the detail didn't go unnoticed. After her initial search

turned up nothing, she looked again, this time deeper into the

suitcase. When Anna ran her hand across the interior lining, she

heard a soft crinkle. Anna discovered a fold in the lining that opened,

revealing some money and an envelope.

In the envelope contained a sloppily written address and

name. The address was from the same town Beth mentioned the

night before at dinner and the name read "Waters." Anna felt

confident that if the men went to that location, they'd either find

Lilly or have some kind of clue about Beth. Anna spent the next day

trying desperately to reach the detectives.

Both detectives agreed it was worth checking out and they

didn't want to lose any more precious time, but they had to stay

around to be sure Lilly hadn't died in the fire. The death of Lilly's

father had brought them to an all-time low. They had so much

weighing on what he could tell them about Beth and Lilly. They still

couldn't prove he didn't take Lilly, but the FBI and the entire town

of Dyer Arkansas were already sifting through the soil and no

remains except James's had been found, so it was pointless to stick

around any longer.

The detectives planned to drive toward Weshure since there were no flights that flew that way and find a place to rest for the night. Then, come morning, they'd unexpectedly appear on the doorstep of the person whose name appeared on the piece of paper. The element of surprise would give them an upper hand with whoever it was.

Daniel was taking the first stretch of the drive. He liked driving at night. It was comforting to him. He liked how the road was filled with lonely truckers on a path to their next paycheck. When he was a kid and he'd take road trips with his parents, they made a game out of counting trucks. The game was perfect for passing time. It worked when he was a kid, but it wasn't fulfilling enough to do now. Instead, he spent his time searching the radio for a good song.

One song would end and he'd flip the dial for his next tune. The search words on the knob had worn away from his constant fumbling with it. It wasn't long, though, before his partner's snoring filled the car. Daniel couldn't help but laugh at the sight of his partner's face pressed up against the window next to him. His mouth dangled open while the horrible growling sound flowed from it. He was now glad they hit the road instead of resting at home. At least Frank's wife would get some sleep tonight, he thought jokingly to himself.

Being Frank's partner was rewarding. Daniel was adopted and an only child, so Frank became his family, inviting him to every function, making Daniel embrace a new concept of family. His parents lived in South Carolina and Daniel was growing more and more distant from them. It wasn't intentional. He simply worked too much. He was due for a visit, though, so he mentally planned ongoing to visit them soon. For now, though, the job and Frank were his life.

Daniel was hesitant at the start to begin a friendship with Frank, but before long, he enjoyed the idea of an extended family. He couldn't wait to one day find the right girl and settle down himself and have kids. It wasn't going to happen anytime soon; he was too engrossed in his work. There was potential, though. Daniel had developed a soft spot for Frank's sister.

She was recently divorced and was spending a lot of time at Frank's house. Daniel didn't see the connection coming, but there was an attraction brewing between them. Daniel hadn't yet entertained the idea of discussing it with Frank. He didn't want to spoil the friendship they had or their working relationship. So, for now, he'd just let the tiny flames spark until the time was right for more. If the time ever came, he thought. He drove on, while ideas bounced through his mind like ping-pong balls, never staying on one for longer than a few minutes.

Daniel pulled the car over into a Motel 8 parking lot. The night was balmy. Daniel opened his car door in silence, trying not to wake his partner. He stretched his limbs and felt his muscles complain under his skin. It was a relief to be able to move about again. The car was such a confining space. He walked inside the quiet motel office and rang the bell. An old man emerged from a room nestled to the left of the counter.

"Hello, what can I do you for?" asked the man as he approached the counter. His feet moved slowly, visibly pained with aching muscles.

Daniel smiled at the man, who reminded him of his adopted grandfather. "I need two rooms, please." He tapped the counter as an afterthought came to mind. "Joined rooms please, if you have them."

The man turned and faced the selection of room keys that hung from hooks behind him. A finger thoughtfully found his upper lip as he contemplated the request. "You're in luck," he said as he plucked two keys from their place and jiggled them in his hand.

"Great," replied Daniel as he pulled out his wallet. He produced his credit card, set it on the counter, sliding it toward the man.

The man took it eagerly and looked up briefly as he keyed in information into the computer. "You're all set." He placed a tiny hotel map down on the counter and circled the room numbers. "Your rooms are here," he said as he pointed to the map. "We have vending machines and ice two rooms down to the left,"

"Thank you," said Daniel as he grabbed the waiting keys. He turned, walking from the tiny lobby, embracing the damp night air. Approaching the car, he saw Frank was still sound asleep. His heart warmed at the sight and a gentle smile rose on his face. He'd listened to Frank snore for the last two hours and he couldn't put his ears through the torment any longer. He clicked the lock on the door and pulled it open. Reaching into the car, he smacked his partner on the chest. "Get up, Sleeping Beauty."

Frank woke with a start as Daniel poked at his arm persistently. Briefly he sat stunned as he wiped the sleep from his eyes. He fumbled to gather his phone and belongings that rested on his lap. "You were supposed to wake me in an hour so I could drive," said Frank through a yawn.

Daniel threw his friend the keys to his room.

"I didn't want to wake you. You were drooling all over the window and there was no way I was going to sit my ass down in that slobbery mess," Daniel grinned. "We have joined rooms 1F and 1E. Wake me at 7:00. Then we will go pay this Mrs. Waters a visit."

He eyed his partner, who was clumsily aiming toward his assigned room. Daniel couldn't help but smirk while his partner fumbled to unlock the motel room door.

Tomorrow held possibilities for them, possibilities that he couldn't begin to allow to penetrate his mind. If he did, lying in bed would be useless. He needed to give himself one night with no thoughts to suffocate him, so when he closed the door and fell into bed, he refused even the simplest idea entry into his psyche, shutting himself down completely from the world while the Sand Man took him into the shadows.

***

Morning came swiftly. The sun seeped leisurely into the room, nudging gently at Daniel. He could feel himself being beckoned by the sun's warmth. As his mind jumped on the journey into wakefulness, he became aware of himself. He felt rested at last.

With energized hands, he reached for his cell phone to check the time. He felt relief that he hadn't overslept by much. It was 7:15 A.M. and he noticed Frank didn't wake him as promised. It was then he saw the note by his bedside table. Frank came in as promised, but gave him twenty more minutes to sleep while he conjured up coffee across the street.

Daniel set the note down and carried himself to the bathroom, where he prepared for the waiting day. The prospects raced over and over in his mind. He stared at himself in the mirror, pleased that the weariness that was etched across his face yesterday had subsided, at least, for the time being. His brown eyes had a resemblance of their youth once again. But he feared before the day's end, all the anguish would resurface abruptly for another show.

He threw the shower curtain open and turned the water all the way up. He wanted to scorch the doubt out of his body so he could hold to the new found hope.

Chapter 22

Dr. Stevens was about to trade shifts with his colleague when his cell phone rang. He answered it and was greeted by a female voice. The caller identified herself as Dr. Owens, the doctor in Oklahoma he'd called the night before.

His pulse quickened as he pressed the phone closer. Why was he surprised it was a woman and not a man? For some reason he'd decided Dr. Owens was a man. He dismissed his bewilderment with a snap, welcoming the timely return call. She was the third one to return his call and the one he was anticipating the most. So far, the others had turned up nothing. His heart beat fiercely.

"Ah, yes, Dr. Owens. I'm so glad you returned my call."

The woman's voice was calm, yet guarded. This didn't surprise him. He'd been faced with doctors who were uncertain when contacted by other doctors. Patient doctor confidentiality always put a strain on their openness. He hastily explained who he was and his connection to Beth Waters. He was beginning to feel silly about why he contacted her. He realized now his explanation had to seem a little odd.

"To be quite honest, I don't know if there's some kind of association between you and Beth, but she garbled your name last night or someone with the name 'Dr. Owens' as she stumbled between unconscious and consciousness." He paused briefly as he chose his words with care. "I simply wanted to see if you knew her. Perhaps you treated her in the past?" He questioned further. He didn't expect her to admit she knew Beth.

There was a long pause on the line as the woman seemed to digest his words. After what seemed to last an eternity, she spoke. "I do recall Beth, Dr. Stevens, but I'm afraid I can't conduct such an interview over the phone. Would you be willing to pay me a visit?" There was a sense of urgency in her next words, and Dr. Steven's flesh prickled. "I think there are a few things you should know about Beth."

He was overjoyed that he'd made a match between the doctors on his list and his patient, Beth. The words from the woman on the other line battered him. He hadn't anticipated such a response, and he knew he needed to act on her suggestion. Her words confirmed there was more to Beth than anyone had projected. The idea of leaving Beth troubled him, but he didn't see any way around it. He was too busy with his thoughts to notice several moments of silence had passed. He stumbled forward with his reply, "Certainly. I can come see you."

"I no longer practice. Would you be comfortable coming to my house?" The question hung between them for a moment. "Also, it's crucial that you don't hesitate. I need you to come now. It's quite urgent," she warned.

Hearing the warning in her voice, Dr. Stevens wasn't about to say no, even though he was exhausted from his shift. He immediately agreed and pulled out a notepad, jotting down her address. He understood why she wouldn't tell him anything over the phone. He knew what it was like to be a doctor. In that profession, people don't just share information over the phone, unless they are entirely certain of the person's identity. He also had to consider who his patient was and the spotlight that was already on her case. He had to be positive Dr. Owens was who she claimed to be. It wouldn't be long before she'd enlighten him fully. He felt certain of that.

After Dr. Stevens disconnected the call, he gathered his belongings and left the hospital. He decided not to tell anyone where he was going as he didn't want to take the chance of the press being alerted to a possible lead in the investigation. Once he knew more, he'd notify the detectives on the case. The idea of a long drive wasn't inviting, but he believed it would be worth the lack of sleep in the end. He was desperate to find out more about Beth.

Chapter 23

The two detectives pulled up in front of the house. It sat nestled off

the road, down a deep driveway. Trees lined the perimeter, keeping

the house out of sight. The only way they knew the house existed

was by the mailbox near the road. A storm was rolling in from the

north. Bleak clouds swarmed in the distance while thunder growled

around them.

The hair on Daniel's arms rose, electrified by the current in

the air. A chill spread through him, regardless of the hot summer

day. He couldn't shake his apprehension as he eyed the dilapidated

farm house before him. He turned to Frank as he placed his gun in

the waistband of his pants, hidden from view. They exchanged

knowing glances. It was a "here we go again" moment. Frank shared

the same face of concern as he, too, eyed the storm closing in.

There were times being a police officer was difficult,

knowing full well that you had to go where no one else would. You

had to face all that was dark and unforgiving in the world. It was

your job to be brave, even when everything within your soul warned you to run the other way. You had to ignore it because it was your job.

The two men walked forward in unison along the pebbled path that led to the house steps, creeping closer to the waiting house and the unknown occupants within.

Before they had a chance to ascend the porch steps, the door to the house creaked open, and a woman stepped out. She glared at the detectives. Both men stalled on the steps, unsure what to expect from the woman who approached them. Her faded blonde hair was swept up in a perfect bun. Her lips were pinched in thin, cold lines. Even though she was older, there was a certain hint to the beauty she once held.

"May I help you boys?" she asked as the front door slammed behind her. She pressed her feet firmly in place, halting them from coming any further. Daniel tried to disarm the woman with a calm voice. "Are you Mrs. Waters?"

Frank stepped a few feet back, distancing himself from Daniel, just enough to give him some options in case the woman or someone else did something stupid. He wasn't taking any chances.

The woman looked shocked by the question. He wasn't sure if it was the shock of them being there, or disbelief that they knew her name. She didn't have to answer the question. The answer was displayed absentmindedly on her face. Her blue eyes returned an icy stare.

"Yes," she reluctantly agreed. "What do you need of me?" Her eyes shifted slowly between the two of them.

Daniel took a step forward, trying to lessen the distance between him and the woman. He threw his right hand up in greeting, trying to reassure her that they meant her no harm.

"Does the name Beth Waters mean anything to you?" he said. He watched as his words made their mark. He could see that she was uncomfortable with his inquiry. Hearing her reply wasn't necessary. He knew the answer already, so he changed his tone. "Your daughter Beth sent us to contact you." The deceitful words crawled from his mouth. "There's been an incident with your granddaughter and she wanted you to know."

Confusion washed over the woman's face for a fleeting moment and then rage replaced it. "I haven't spoken to my daughter in twelve years. She left in anger and never returned. Why should I give a damn about her or a child of hers?" she stated flatly. The coldness in her tone radiated across her face.

Daniel hadn't anticipated such a frigid response, but if there was one area he was unsure of, it was the parent and child relationship. He tried his best to connect with her, nonetheless. He thought back to his childhood and remembered the resentment he felt from bouncing around from foster home to foster home. As a result, he didn't consider himself close with his adoptive parents, but he doubted they'd ever refer to him with such venom. He tried to put on his best perceptive front by nodding knowingly.

"I understand your anger, Ma'am, teenagers can be difficult, but your granddaughter has been kidnapped, and we had to let you know." Daniel was trying to shift his approach. He needed to give the woman a reason to forget about her anger over her daughter and instead, focus on the needs of her grandchild that was out there somewhere in the world.

The lady paused briefly as she contemplated the situation. "I suppose we do have quite the situation now, don't we?" She folded her arms and leaned against the wall behind her. She offered a cunning smile. "Would you like to come in for something to drink so we can discuss the issue?" She straightened up off the wall and placed her thin hand on the screen door.

Daniel was grateful for the change of heart, even if it lacked conviction. He desperately wanted to get into the house so he could look around for signs of Lilly. He didn't want any surprises, so he stopped briefly to ask, "Would your husband be okay with that?"

She paused briefly as she opened the screen door. Her icy blue eyes turned soft for just a moment. "My husband, my dear, died a few years back. It's just me and my daughter here on this land," she added dryly as she stepped into the house. She crossed her arms briefly as she turned to face the men; the screen door leaned gently against her hip. "You two coming in or not?" She didn't wait for an answer as she walked inside, leaving the detectives no choice but to follow behind.

The house was spacious and modestly kept. She indicated for the men to follow her into the dark hunter green dining room to the right of the entryway. A long table took up the length of the room and a faded embroidered tablecloth and a bowl of plastic fruit covered the center. The walls held an assortment of framed art and photographs.

Mrs. Waters indicated for them to take a seat around the table while she went to get them something to drink. After she left the room, Daniel and Frank took the chance to soak up as many details as they could. Beyond the dining room was what appeared to be a living room, and across from the dining room was an office or den. The kitchen couldn't be seen, but based on the sounds of running water coming from the back of the house, Daniel figured it was probably in that direction.

Frank and Daniel moved in opposite directions around the room, checking out pictures and other items. There was no telling what they'd find, but they needed to uncover something. At this point, there didn't seem to be any sign of Lilly, but there was a second floor that needed to be considered.

Daniel turned away from the wall he was exploring when he heard the lady return. She was holding a tray with cups filled with coffee, tiny canisters of sugar and cream. She wore the same pinched expression from moments earlier. Placing the tray on the table, she indicated for the detectives to sit with her. Daniel thanked her as he approached the table. Frank, on the other hand, requested a trip to her washroom.

Mrs. Waters eyed him cautiously, but reluctantly guided him to the hallway. "It's the second door on the right, down the hall," she instructed.

Frank thanked her with a sheepish grin. Daniel knew the woman was cautiously suspicious based on the twinge of distrust in her eyes, so he turned on his puppy dog charm. There were few times his charm failed, and he had to be sure this would not be one of them. He started off with small compliments on her appearance. He turned up the heat by making each smile he gave count.

"Your home is beautiful," he lied. He actually found it dreary.

She grinned as she poured the coffee into three cups. "You're a terrible liar, detective," she stated coyly. "My husband has been gone a few years, and I lack what it takes to keep such a large home in shape." A twinkle suddenly filled her eyes as she stared at Daniel.

He could swear she was beginning to flirt with him. He'd never been flirted with by a woman her age. Part of him was flattered, and the other part was trying to stay professional. The latter lasted only a moment, however, when he decided flirting back might keep her distracted. He found no shame in doing everything it took to get some answers.

Meanwhile, Frank was walking slowly through the house, listening intently as he passed doors for some kind of movement from inside. Big houses gave him the creeps. There were so many doors and halls. Older style homes didn't have the open floor plans of the styles today. You had to go through one closed door to enter the next room and, given its size, there was no way to visually cover this house quickly, so he was depending heavily on what his ears could pick up. There was little to be heard, though.

Beyond the bathroom was another bedroom, but he couldn't go much further past it for fear of being seen. That room was also empty. As he passed through the hall, he glanced briefly at the photographs on the wall. He heard a dull thump from upstairs that startled him. He ushered himself toward the bathroom, where he tucked himself inside. He wasn't sure what the noise was, but he could only assume it was the daughter Mrs. Waters mentioned. Standing in the bathroom, he was unsure what to do next. He opened the medicine cabinet and sifted through its contents. He didn't know what the hell he expected to find, but he searched it quickly, nonetheless. Once he had looked in every corner, he was satisfied there was nothing to be found. He flushed the toilet and turned on the sink and washed his hands, just in case this house was typical of older homes and the water could be heard from other rooms. It was then that he realized he may have stumbled upon something interesting in the hall. He could kick himself for not realizing it sooner. Stepping back into the hall, he double checked.

Daniel was halfway through his coffee when he was running out of things to discuss. He started off with small talk, but he was ready to dig up some information, so he put a halt to the idle chat. "You said you and your daughter had a fight. May I ask what about?"

The woman's lips left their flirty stance, and she placed her coffee cup down gently. The cup rattled.

Mrs. Waters couldn't hide the distaste in her voice. "Beth was a typical teenager. She thought she had all the answers she needed to get her through her life. It wasn't a pretty departure, but I decided I had no choice but to let her go." Her words danced from her lips as though rehearsed. Perhaps she'd thought of her and her daughter's final moments many times. Daniel could only suspect. If he had a child who'd left so suddenly, he couldn't imagine the feeling and the thoughts that would keep him awake at night. *Time may or may not heal the wound of a child leaving in such a way*, he thought as he considered his next question.

"She never sent word about your granddaughter?" The question was stated calmly.

He noticed a slight twinge in the corner of her eye. He could see the question bothered her, but she sat coyly. "To be honest with you, detective, I had no idea I was a grandmother." The statement was unadorned, but the weight of it struck Daniel like an anvil being dropped in front of his face. He believed her. It was a combination of her words and the look within her eyes that told him she had no idea about Lilly.

Chapter 24

When Beth woke, she was unsure of where she was. Then, the familiar smell of antiseptic and bleach filled her nostrils. She knew she was back in the hospital. But why? Her body ached all over and she felt weakened to her core. She didn't know what day it was. *How long have I been here?* Her hand reached toward her abdomen. Her pregnant belly always gave her comfort when she felt alone, but she didn't find it swollen as expected. The sensation of finding her stomach smaller brought panic over her, but then she remembered the events of the day before. She completely gave in to the fear. The last words she remembered hearing before she fell into darkness echoed in her mind. *"I think the baby is dead."* A coldness filled her body as the idea of never holding her baby found its way into her thoughts. A swollen tear slid down her cheek and rested on her upper lip. Stoically, she sat. No thoughts could get past the resounding words. The room began to spin, but she forced her eyes to focus and threw her covers off. "No! No, no, I want my baby!"

Absentmindedly, she reached for the wires that hooked her body up to the machines and yanked them from her arms. The pain was agonizing, but she was glad to be free. A loud screech beeped from the room, but she ignored it as she swung her legs over the bed towards the floor. At this point, no one had responded to the nagging beeps coming from her room. She slowly lowered her feet to the cold floor. Her legs collapsed beneath her. The constant whining from the machines was splitting her mind in two. She crawled towards the back of the hospital bed, searching for the cords that brought the sound life and she tore them from the wall in one hard yank.

Her legs were beginning to tingle, suggesting life was returning to them. She crawled on her hands and knees back to the side of the bed and pulled to a standing position. She had to find her baby. Her legs trembled under her weight, but she refused to allow them to collapse again. Beth inched towards her hospital room door. Pain gripped every muscle within her body and she fought the tears that seeped from the deepest part of her.

She strained when she tugged on the door. The lights from the hall were dim, suggesting it was night. She followed the sounds of distant laughter and conversation. The hall appeared to shrink and elongate as she stepped forward. She was grateful for the railings on

174

the walls. Her hands shook as they gripped the rails, but she held tight as she pushed forward. Pure determination shoved her onward.

The talking grew louder. Before long, Beth discovered the nurse's desk and the two women who were chatting away as she approached. The second they saw her; she could see shock grow on their faces. One turned to check the monitors that were blinking red, indicating that an alarm sounded that they hadn't heard. Concern filled their faces. Neither one of them spoke. They just stood there staring, uncertain what to do next.

"I want my baby," Beth stammered in an aching whisper. She was seconds from falling to the floor, but she held strong, trying to refocus her eyes on the two women. Her voice seemed to shock them into action. The tall one rushed toward her while the other one reached for a wheelchair that sat against the wall. She yanked it open and wheeled behind Beth, who sat without being told.

"I just want my baby," she repeated under her breath.

The two women didn't argue. They made sure Beth was secure in the seat and then pushed her towards the nursery.

The nursery was dark, with only gentle floor and ceiling lights. There was just enough light for Beth to see tiny little pods that encased sleeping babies. The nurses wheeled her on in silence, past one sleeping baby after another. Beth counted four babies before they stopped next to one. The nurse pushed the brake down on the chair and Beth was certain the baby they stopped in front of was her very own.

The second nurse walked around to the sleeping baby and whispered, "Would you like to hold her?"

Beth heard her words, but the moment didn't seem real. She'd waited so long for this minute and it was actually about to happen. She couldn't speak. A single tear streaked down her face. She nodded slowly at first, and then with more conviction.

The nurse lifted the baby gently and carried it to Beth. It was swaddled in a soft, pink blanket and Beth knew it must be a girl. She stared in awe at the tiny creature that instantly captured her heart. She pulled the little girl closer to her, embracing her as tightly as she dared. There was no happier moment than she could remember. There was no feeling on earth that could possibly compare to the love she was feeling right then.

One of the nurse's voices filled the silence that had graced the hall. Her voice was soft and sweet and Beth was pleased to hear the message. "She is doing very well, considering her sudden delivery."

Beth turned her eyes toward the woman. "When was she born? I don't even know what day it is." She silently feared the answer. She hoped it wasn't too long ago.

"It has been two and a half days since you gave birth," the nurse replied gently as she tucked the tiny foot that had escaped from the fleece.

Beth was astonished by the news. Her mouth fell open. *Had it really been two days since she'd given birth?* She turned her interest back to the petite baby she was cradling in her arms. The little girl had thin blonde strands of hair. She was sleeping, so her eyes were a mystery. But she had Beth's full red lips and long lashes.

The moment didn't seem real. She wanted to pinch herself to check if she was dreaming. Happiness was finally a part of her world. She gazed at the baby. Love radiated over them, and she didn't care about anything else. The world could spin uncontrollably all it wanted. She was looking at the only thing in her life worth living for. She sat for several moments in silence taking in every feature of her daughter, trying to memorize them.

The nurse cut through the silence with her soft voice. "She still needs a name. Have you thought of any?"

Beth looked up for a moment as she contemplated the question. She hadn't decided on a name yet. Part of her was embarrassed by the revelation. She thought about the question, taking her time to answer. "I like the name Lilly," she replied with a pensive smile.

The nurse looked at her oddly, as if confused by the statement. It took her several moments to respond, but Beth was too distracted to notice.

"Do you think that's a good idea?"

Chapter 25

When Frank returned to the dining room, he found Daniel standing as if he was ready to go. Frank was still trying to calm his racing heartbeat, and his head was spinning out of control. There was no simple way to wrap his mind around it. He couldn't bring himself to look eye to eye with the lady who was searching for him with as much intent as his partner. He wasn't going to mention anything to Daniel until they were safely out of the house and in the privacy of the car. With strained effort, he kept a poker face and stepped forward to extend his hand to Mrs. Waters, glad their meeting was about to come to an end.

Daniel was eyeing his partner, trying to get a read on him. Frank wasn't revealing anything, though. His colleague was calm and collected with the exception of the small twitch over his right eye. To an untrained eye, it wasn't noticeable, but Daniel knew his partner well enough to know something had him lit up.

They bade their goodbyes and walked from the house. The air surrounding them was thick and ominous. The first drops of rain spit down upon them. The drops were small, but the menacing blackness above hinted they were in the calm before the storm. The promise of a battle was evident. Daniel clicked the button that released the locks on the doors and they each climbed into the car.

Daniel turned to his co-worker as he placed the key in the ignition. "So, what is it? I know you know something." Frank reached over his shoulder and grabbed his seat belt. His eyes slowly returned their attention back to his partner. "We have two choices. We get a search warrant or we forget that and somehow manage to get back into that house any way we can."

Frank's words felt like a sharp slap in the face. His gut flipped and twisted.

"What did you see?" The question hung heavily between them. The answer would determine the urgency with which they'd move forward.

"That woman is lying about something. She claims she hasn't seen her daughter, and that could be true, but she knows about Lilly," he added confidently.

Daniel began driving, and he wished he hadn't. He was feeling nauseous with each detail revealed. "What do you mean?"

He glanced at his partner, wishing the answer would come quicker. His patience was growing thin.

"While I was walking toward the bathroom, I noticed something. I didn't know what I'd seen until I was in the bathroom, so I went back for a second look," Frank explained as he brushed his hands through his thick black hair.

"You won't fucking believe what was hanging on the wall in the hall." It wasn't a question, but a statement. Fury radiated from his face. "If she doesn't know Lilly exists, why the hell does she have a picture of her hanging on her wall?" he asked in an unwavering tone.

His words lingered between them.

"That's not all." He stopped and waited for Daniel to give him his undivided attention. "The picture isn't a drawing, and Lilly is the same age she is now and…" he let his words stretch out as far as he could. "She is wearing the exact same outfit she was kidnapped in."

Daniel nearly swerved off the road. What Frank just said didn't make any sense. If that was true, then Lilly had to be in the same house they'd just left. They were right there within a few feet of her. He could kick himself. She was so close, and they didn't even know it. Not only that, he totally bought the woman's story. He thought for sure she was telling the truth when she said she didn't know she had a granddaughter. He was completely baffled how he couldn't have missed all the clues. He must be exhausted or losing his touch! Anger rose under his skin. He was infuriated over the brazen lie she'd told him. He wanted nothing more than to go back and throw her up against the wall like he did Ben, the Walgreen's manager. But he wouldn't.

He needed to end this now and correctly. He didn't want any part of the case to come back on them. He wanted the woman to go to jail for a very long time, and he wouldn't do anything that would jeopardize the case. For Lilly's sake, he needed to set aside all of his emotions and get her home safely so she could live out her childhood the way she deserved. He owed her that much. If it took his last breath, he'd make sure she made it back home.

Chapter 26

Dr. Stevens was driving when the call came in from the hospital saying that Beth finally woke up. His colleague was there watching over her care. He was grateful for that. He was already more than halfway to Dr. Owens' and he didn't want to turn back, but he was quite concerned with the details of her behavior after she woke up.

Two nurses found her stumbling to the nurse's station, demanding to see her baby. Beth ripped her IV from her arm in the process. That information wasn't the most startling detail. The nurses reported that Beth was thinking of naming the baby Lilly. Dr. Stevens didn't know if that was an indication that Beth was giving up on Lilly, or perhaps something far worse. He wished he could be in two places at once. He wanted to be the one caring for her right now, but he reasoned with himself that in many ways he was.

His research and a hunch warned him that something was wrong, something that he wasn't equipped to diagnose. He had to get to Dr. Owens to see if his hunch could be validated in any way. Dr. Stevens ordered a complete psych evaluation on Beth and promised that he'd return as soon as he'd made a connection. He explained that he was doing research on Beth and he couldn't head back yet. Steven's ordered the staff to keep her isolated for now and not to allow the baby to room with her until he knew more about her mental state. His foot pressed harder on the gas as he drove forward with even more determination.

He was exhausted, but adrenaline drove him forward. The clouds opened up and rain poured down on the windshield, making it difficult to see. He was one of the few cars on the road.

He was closing in on his destination, and he couldn't help but wonder what the doctor would share. The rain grew thicker as he pushed forward on the abandoned road. The houses stretched farther apart. He approached a car pulled off along the road and thought for a moment about stopping. The two men within it seemed to be deeply engrossed in a discussion. He slowed as he passed them, but the driver waved him on, so he decided they were okay.

It wasn't long before he found the house he was looking for. It sat nestled off of the main road. A long driveway stretched deep into the property. He parked his car and waited. He wasn't sure what he was waiting for; the rain was in no way close to letting up, so he threw the door open and ran for the house, throwing his brown trench coat over his head as he ran.

Eagerly, he took the porch steps two at a time, grateful when he made his way under the awning. Lightning struck above him, illuminating the sky around him. He shook the excess rain off as he pushed the doorbell. A gentle ding sounded from within and he waited, the anticipation growing.

It was several moments before a woman appeared before him. He couldn't make out her face through the gray screen door. It was her voice that reached him first. There was a gentle coolness that filled it.

"Oh my. I was expecting someone else. May I help you?" she said.

"Yes. I'm Dr. Stevens. You asked me to drop by. I'm so sorry I'm late. I got a late start," he apologized.

"Oh yes, Dr. Stevens," the woman replied as she pushed the screen door open, revealing her face to him. "I'm so glad you could come. Won't you come in?" She stepped aside to allow Dr. Stevens' passage into the house. Lighting struck once again outside, sending the indoor lights into a slow flicker.

"My, it's really kicking up out there," said the woman as she stuck out her hand. "Let me take your coat so you can get comfortable." He turned, allowing her to remove his coat.

"Thank you." He withdrew his arms from his coat, releasing it to her grasp. He watched her as she hung it on a coat rack near the entryway. She wasn't quite what he'd anticipated. He expected an older woman, someone who looked old enough to be retired. She was perhaps in her 40s or early 50s. There were lines etched on her face, but there was also a sense of beauty that remained. She looked classy, and relatively untouched by time. Her hair looked like she'd just run her fingers through it. The loose long strands framed her face adding to her mature exquisiteness.

The house was dimly lit, releasing a gentle glow. He took a quick look around and noticed a set of red suitcases by the stairs.

"I'm sorry, doctor. Am I keeping you from anything?"

The woman seemed caught off guard by his query, and then she turned her eyes in the direction his eyes indicated. She smiled coyly as she waved off the idea.

"Oh. No, not in the least. My daughter and I were going to go visit family for the weekend, but we're going to wait for the storm to pass before we hit the road, so your visit is no bother to us." She gave a gentle laugh as she placed her hand over her throat, fumbling with the necklace that rested there. "Please, come into the living room and sit down. You must be exhausted from the drive, and please, call me Victoria," she added with a smile. She motioned him to walk with her past what appeared to be a dining room, towards the back of the house.

He followed her, all the while catching quick glances around the house. "I appreciate you letting me visit. I'm quite concerned about my patient," he stated as he sat on the couch where she invited him to sit. The light in the room was much brighter than the entryway he'd walked through. He was finally able to get a good look at her.

She had light blonde hair and stunning blue eyes. He was quite taken by her. There was a commanding presence about her that made him feel connected in some way, but regardless of how he was feeling about her, he had to begin the task at hand and that was discovering what was going on with his patient.

"So, about Beth Waters, what was it you thought I should know?"

Victoria sat across from him in a deep green cushioned chair. She scooped her skirt under her as she crossed her ankles to the side. "Oh, forgive me, doctor. I've forgotten my manners. Let me go and get you some coffee. How does that sound?" she asked with a sweet smile.

Dr. Stevens wasn't thinking about coffee, but he could definitely use some, so he nodded. She stood as soon as he accepted her offer and left him sitting on the couch alone. He was never one to sit idly by very well, so he stood and circulated the room. The walls were covered in photographs and framed documents, such as awards and her doctorate degrees. He could hear the gentle clank from the kitchen, reminding him not to be too nosy because she could easily return at any moment.

It was then that he heard a soft whimper from behind him. He turned to find a little girl standing there. He was startled at first, but he didn't want to frighten her, so he pasted a smile on his face.

"You must be Dr. Owens' daughter. I'm a friend of hers. What's your name?" he asked in a hushed whisper as he took a step towards the little girl.

She stood gazing between him and the door that led to the kitchen. "She isn't my mommy," she replied in a soft voice.

Dr. Stevens didn't quite know if he'd heard her correctly or not. He took a small step towards her and kneeled down, trying to reach her level. He couldn't tell how old she was, but he was guessing her to be around four.

"What do you mean, she isn't your mommy? Is she your auntie?" he inquired further.

The little girl continued to stare at him. There was a sense of nervousness around her. She seemed afraid of being caught talking to him.

"She isn't my mommy," she repeated once again is a hushed whisper.

He tried to scoot towards her, but she stepped back at the same time.

"No. Wait. I'm not going to hurt you," he stated as he tried to convince her with gentle words that he wasn't a bad guy. She turned and ran from the room in the direction she came from, and at the same time Victoria emerged from behind the kitchen door.

She halted, frozen mid-step as the little girl fled from the room. Dr. Stevens turned to see her slam her gaping mouth closed. She moved forward as he stood and walked back to the chair and sat down. He watched as she placed the tray on the coffee table.

Victoria let a beaming grin cross her face and an apologetic twinkle in her eyes followed suit. "That's my daughter," she explained. "Please don't pay her any mind. She isn't quite well in the head. If you know what I mean."

Dr. Stevens connected the child's behavior with Victoria's brief explanation. She handed him a cup of coffee. He returned her kind smile and sipped on the steaming cup of coffee she'd made him. He held it, letting it warm his hands. Never one to drink coffee while it was piping hot, he set it on the table in front of him. He sat back in his chair. "So, you were saying that I needed to know something about Beth. Could you explain to me what I need to know?"

She gazed at him cautiously before she began her tale. "Beth was a patient of mine many years ago," she stated as she walked toward a window that faced the back of the house.

"You know, I never thought I'd ever hear her name again. How is it you said you found me?" she asked as she stared out the back window.

Dr. Stevens went over the details of how Beth came into his care and what he knew about her so far. He went into detail about Lilly and the delivery of Beth's new little girl. He finally arrived at the detail of Beth's recovery and how Dr. Owens came to be discovered.

In that time, Dr. Owens made her way back to the chair across from him and sat down. She folded her arms as she listened to him recall the information.

"So, no one else knows about me?" she asked as a smile crossed her face.

"No. I left as soon as we spoke and I didn't want to make a big production about it," he informed her as he reached for his cup once again. It had cooled some, making it easier for him to drink. There was a long moment of silence as he took several sips. Then Victoria started talking. She had an all too familiar serious doctor demeanor about her. "Let me ask you this, Dr. Stevens. You're here because you're trying to figure out what is wrong with your patient."

He was expecting a question, but it was a statement, and he noticed a peculiar kind of iciness in her tone. He took another sip from his cup before he said, "Yes. I believe she is displaying some signs of post-traumatic stress. I'm not sure whether I'm right or not, but in my research, I've found that pregnant women sometimes recall trauma from the past during pregnancy. It's a rare condition, but Beth has already proven to dance on the rare condition side of things." He could feel his body beginning to warm from the coffee. Sweat emerged in tiny bubbles on his upper lip.

"So, you think her pregnancy was making her recall information? What kind of information?" the woman asked.

"Well, she mumbled your name in her sleep, for one. She'd mentioned previously not having any doctors and then she mentioned your name. There are other details too that just seem odd, so I figured I'd investigate. I've discovered pregnant women's hormones can release a chemical in their brains that trigger memory recall. It's my belief that Beth is one of those women," he added, quite pleased with himself. "I also believe now that the baby has been delivered, if I don't find the problem, her repressed memory could return to wherever she's been hiding it." He let out a laugh as he realized how weird it may sound. "I mean, it's just a hunch. I don't know for sure what will happen," he added. The woman sitting in front of him crossed one leg over the other.

The sweat had formed droplets that were about to cascade downward, and he reached for his collar in hope of releasing some of the heat his body was generating. It didn't do any good. Part of him was in a panic. Fear sizzled under his skin. His eyes jittered back and forth as his vision waned between blurriness and darkness. The woman just sat and stared. He noticed a small sense of mockery cross her face, as if she was silently pleased by what she was seeing. His attention swayed toward the coffee cup. The reality smashed into him. He felt certain Victoria had put something in his cup. A sensation of horror washed over him as his symptoms worsened. He knew he was moments from blacking out, and was afraid once he did pass out, he'd never wake up again.

Chapter 27

Beth was annoyed by all the questions the psychologist was asking. It started the morning she woke up and went to find her baby. She just didn't understand what all the fuss was about. The constant pesky questions had her feeling on edge. She wished the doctors would simply say what they meant; instead, they'd ask her a question, jot something down on their clipboards and eye one another as if they were speaking in a silent secret language. They even removed her baby from the room and refused to let Beth see her until 'all their concerns were appeased.' They'd left the room to discuss some things and Beth was waiting for them to return and continue the little chat.

She sat staring at the photograph of her tiny baby. She couldn't believe she'd created such a beautiful life. The separation was killing her. She couldn't wait for all of this to be over. She just wanted her life back. Her hands reached for the blanket that covered her, twisting and turning it around and around. All the built-up frustration was strangling its way down into her fingers. Her knuckles were white from the strain. Just then, the door to her room opened, and she released the blanket from her vice-like grip. She didn't want them to see how ticked off she was. They didn't need any more fuel to keep their fire burning.

The two doctors walked toward her, returning to their seats by her bed. One was a man, and the other was a woman. These two were accountable for keeping her prisoner and away from her baby. She tried desperately to hide her animosity, though. Her game plan was to remain calm and collected the best she could in order to convince them she was healthy enough to care for her daughter. Then, when she was far enough out of reach, she'd give them a piece of her mind.

"I don't understand why you guys are acting like this. I'm perfectly fine. I already told you that," Beth stated flatly. She turned her gaze from one doctor to the next, pleading with her eyes.

"Beth, we're just trying to calm our concerns. You told one of the nurses that you wanted to name your baby Lilly and we're very uncertain why you would want to do that," stated the male doctor that stood before her.

Beth threw her hands up in exasperation. "I don't understand why it's such a big deal. I like the name Lilly."

"Beth, what about your daughter, Lilly? She's been missing four days. Don't you feel naming your new baby Lilly would be a step in the direction of replacing her?" inquired the female doctor. "For us, it indicates separation from your former life and your daughter, Lilly. It raises a lot of concerns regarding your state of mind. We're afraid you've given up on finding Lilly alive," explained the woman. She hugged her clip board and nudged her glasses thoughtfully upward on her face.

"You guys keep saying that," replied Beth through clenched teeth. This time, her anger boiled to the top. *How many times would she have to defend herself to them?* she thought, smothering annoyance.

"I don't know why you guys are treating me like I'm crazy! I've told you a million times, this baby is the only Lilly I have." She threw the covers off of her body and lunged out of the bed. Both doctors stood and backed up a pace. Beth reached for her clothes. She ripped her hospital gown off, disregarding any modesty, and replaced it with a dress that Anna had brought her. She was furious. Getting out of there before they could force her to stay was all she could think about.

"Beth, you need to sit down," demanded the male doctor.

"I have rights," argued Beth as she threw her belongings into a suitcase. "You can't sit there and tell me I'm crazy when nothing you guys are saying makes any sense. I'm taking my baby and we're leaving. You have no right keeping me here." Fury exploded from her.

The female doctor walked slowly towards Beth, trying to calm her while the male doctor reached for the room phone. Beth had no idea who he was calling, but she didn't care. She knew with him distracted she had to take her chance to escape. She grabbed her bag and swung it as hard as she could at the female doctor's face, sending her crashing to the ground. Beth lunged for the door and ran from the room, crashing into a nurse on her way out.

She ran in the direction of the nursery, using the doctor's swipe key she had grabbed on her way out of the room to gain access, but it didn't work. Too late, she realized, psychologists probably didn't need access to the nursery. She banged on the glass for the nurses within to open it, but they just stared at her. One of them smashed her hand down on a button that set off a loud alarm throughout the corridor. Lights flashed above her, distracting her with their loud screams. Then suddenly she saw Anna come up behind her.

"Oh my God, Beth, child. What are you doing?"

Beth looked at Anna and silently pleaded for her to help. Tears streamed down her face. Beth could see the two doctors making their way down the hall and they weren't alone. Two security guards were right behind them. She returned her attention back to the nursery and continued to bang on the doors. It was then that Anna intervened as she slammed Beth up to the glass, pinning her against it.

"Beth, you have to calm down. They're going to commit you," she explained. "I'm so sorry, Beth, but as your friend, I'm going to let them. You are out of control. Something has happened. It's probably your hormones all out of balance, but you're going to hurt yourself at this rate." Anna's voice softened. "Please, Beth. Don't do this." Beth began sobbing as the reality of Anna's words sank in. There was nothing more she could do. She sucked in a deep breath and screamed as loud as she could. "Why are you doing this to me?" she begged. "I haven't done anything wrong."

Beth could feel herself being cuffed by the security guard. She kicked and screamed with every ounce of energy she had left in her body. She wasn't going down without a fight.

The two officers lifted her, one took her hands, and the other took her feet and they carried her struggling body through a set of double doors, out of the labor and delivery wing. A nurse came around the corner and jabbed a needle into Beth's arm and within moments, all the fight she had was snuffed out. All she could do was whimper jumbled nonsense. Her mind was slowing to a gentle, slurred mess. She couldn't believe this was happening to her all over again.

Chapter 28

Dr. Stevens woke to find himself flat on his back. Pain radiated from every inch of his body, especially his head. The thumping pulsated from deep within, causing him to wince with each movement he made. At first, he couldn't understand his predicament, and then he recalled the moments just before he passed out.

Dr. Owens was standing over him, her face dimming in and out of focus. Then she spoke the strangest words he'd ever heard. "I can't let you go back to Beth because if you do, you'll make her better and everything I have good going for me will be taken away." *What the hell is she talking about?* He didn't have a chance to respond. His eyes couldn't fight the darkness, and he fell begrudgingly into it.

He didn't know how much time had passed, but he was awake again, and furious to find himself in this situation. He gently rolled himself over onto his knees, taking his time to assess his injuries. There didn't seem to be anything more than a few bumps and bruises. Blood trickled from the side of his head. He fumbled forward in the darkness, searching for anything that would give a clue to his location. The only sound that could be heard was muffled voices and the occasional creak from the ceiling above him. His eyes were slowly adjusting to the darkness, but he decided it was probably as good as it was going to get. He crawled forward, feeling through the darkness until he found a set of stairs. He made his way to his feet and ascended the steps slowly.

Each step caused a scraping sound to fill the air, so he moved as slow as he possibly could, feeling the wall next to the steps for some kind of light switch. He noticed as he crawled up the stairs that the light from under the door made it possible for him to see just a little bit. He was grateful for the soft illumination. He was almost near the top of the steps when he spotted a light switch, but he was afraid to turn it on and call attention to the fact that he was conscious. After several moments of debate, he decided it was worth the risk, so he flicked the switch on. Finally, he could see. He didn't waste time, though; he went right back down the steps so he could get a good sense of where he was. He needed to find something that could be used as a weapon. It was obvious now that he was in the basement of the house. There were boxes and items stored all around him. He rummaged through the shelves and found a flashlight.

Silently, he prayed it would work. There were also batteries in the box next to the flashlight. He pushed the switch, and the flashlight faded on and off. He tightened the top and what was a weak glow became brighter. Turning back toward the steps, he headed back up to turn the light switch off. Once he was back down in the basement, he began searching the room for a weapon. That was when he noticed the storm cellar doors. Silently, he searched for a latch. He found it, but when he pushed on it, it didn't budge. His heart sank. He wasn't going to waste any time, though. He should have known he'd find it locked. The woman was obviously nuts and crazy people were smart and resourceful. She wouldn't have put him somewhere where he could possibly escape. Now it was time for him to become resourceful and smart. He had to figure out how to get out of this situation. He had to get to the police somehow.

He turned his attention back to the cellar, using the flashlight to scan the room. He began reading labels on boxes. One read canned food. Another one read tools. "Bingo," he whispered softly. Ripping open the box, he found a hammer and a pocket knife. He decided the pocket knife would be perfect to hide somewhere on his body and he chose to put several other tools in strategically hidden

202

places, so if she came down and he could get an advantage, she wouldn't see it coming. As he was hiding the hammer under a shelf, he noticed another box. It was labeled Lillian. Immediately, his senses revved up into high gear. He needed to find out what was in that box.

It was sealed, so he used the pocket knife to slice it open. He opened the box with great care. Inside, he found baby blankets folded on top. Gently, he took them out and set them aside. Once the blankets were removed, he found photographs underneath. He held up the flashlight and shined it on the photographs. He'd seen the image before. It was Lilly, the missing daughter of Beth. Her face was unmistakable. He'd seen her image over and over on the news. There was no doubt.

He shuffled the photographs in his hand, taking a close look at each picture. Lilly was about three years old in the first few and then he found some of what appeared to be an eight-year-old Lilly and then a teenage Lilly. It didn't make any sense. Lilly was three now, but the faces in the pictures were relatively unchanged. He had little doubt that they were all Lilly. But, how is that possible, he thought as he set them aside? He searched the box more to see if the contents would reveal something more. He pulled out a little outfit. In his hands, he held a pink jumper dress with lady bugs on it and a turtleneck that also had lady bugs on it. He turned the outfit over and over in his hands and examined it closely. His head spun. He wasn't dreaming. These items were real. What was going on? As he set the outfit aside, some loose papers fell to the ground. Among them was a newspaper clipping.

He picked it up and unfolded it. The bold caption on the paper turned his blood cold. He couldn't believe what he was reading, but it was there, right in front of his face. Everything was beginning to make sense now. All the puzzle pieces he was trying to sort suddenly fell into place. He read the words over and over, but he found no error in their print.

"Have you seen Lillian Beth Strouse?"

Lilly was Beth. There was no doubt in his mind now. The little girl everyone has been searching for didn't even exist, at least, not in the same way everyone believed. He grabbed the news clipping and shoved it in his pocket. This was the only piece of evidence he'd be able to take with him to prove his theory. He turned to see what was creaking from behind him.

When he turned, he was hit by something on the left side of his head. The pain and force of the blunt object sent him flying into the stuff stacked against the cellar wall. A shelf knocked free and it and its contents nearly landed on his head, too, but he was able to dodge them just in time. In the darkness, he could see Dr. Owens holding a shovel.

She threw the shovel aside and reached behind herself, producing a more menacing weapon. The gun wasn't yet aimed at Dr. Stevens, so he threw himself at her with all the force he could manage, trying desperately to grab the gun from her hand. He tripped on a crate and they both fell to the floor. Dr. Stevens could hear his heart beating within his chest as the adrenaline forced it into overdrive. He wondered if this moment would be his final one on earth.

He decided if he was going down, then he'd go down fighting. He lunged forward again and grabbed the woman's wrist as she was taking aim with the gun. He forced all of his body weight onto her, forcing her back into a wall. He thought for a fleeting moment that he finally had the upper hand, but she stomped on his foot and bit his arm.

His flesh ripped open. Blood seeped down the length of his arm. Instead of simply letting go of the woman, he threw her off of him, tossing her against a wall. He noticed the gun fly from her hands, landing somewhere in the stacks of boxes. He felt relieved. She recovered with renewed energy and came at him fighting with an evil strength. Dr. Stevens reached back and swung his fist into her face as hard as he could. Blood splattered across the room as she stumbled backwards. He took the chance to try to flee, but he tripped over the shovel, crashing toward the floor. He kicked the flashlight in the process and it swirled around in circles.

He attempted to get to the hammer he'd hidden, but she was on him within seconds. Stumbling forward, he fell with a crash on top of a plastic crate. The woman was on his back, banging his face into the ground. He tried to lift himself up, but she was kneeling on his arms, keeping him from getting any leverage. He couldn't believe the strength she had. He struggled against her weight, trying to throw her off. Then, just as he was about to get free, he felt something hard slam into his temple. He fell into darkness in the same second. It happened so fast; he didn't even have a chance to take a final breath.

Chapter 29

The detectives sat on the side of the road as they contemplated their options. They didn't want to screw it up. Their cell phones didn't have any service, so they were on their own. They could take the chance and drive to the closest town so they could call in what they knew, but they didn't want to lose sight of their suspect and Lilly. They decided their only option was to hide their car and walk through the fields and sit on the house for a bit for some kind of proof their hunch was right. Fortunately, after about twenty minutes of waiting, the storm passed over and only a trickle of its presence remained. The thunder could still be heard rumbling across the dark sky.

They reached the end of the field and peered through the high grass in the direction of the house.

"Do you see that?" asked Frank.

A silver Mercedes sat in the driveway.

"Yeah, who the hell could that be?" whispered Daniel as he searched for signs of movement from within. The house was completely still though, hinting nothing.

"Dude, I think that's the car that slowed as it passed us a while ago."

"Yeah, I think you're right."

"So, what do we do?" Frank asked.

"I don't know. This changes things. We don't know who that is and things could get out of control." Disappointment layered his voice with doubt. "Let's simmer here for a few minutes and see if someone comes out."

Frank flipped the button on his holster, gaining him quicker access to the gun. They waited for several moments. Neither one of them spoke another word. They crouched on the soggy ground, engrossed in the moment, listening keenly to the night around them, trying to get a sense of the situation. The storm made its way west, but its grumbling could still be heard pounding the distant horizon.

Out of the corner of his eye, Daniel saw movement near the front door. He tapped Frank on the shoulder and nudged him to look in the same direction. Mrs. Waters emerged from within and walked towards the car in her driveway. She opened the door and got in.

"Shit! Do we stop her?" asked Frank, ready to pounce.

At this point she'd already roared the car to life and threw it
into reverse.

"No. If she leaves, we're going in. She doesn't have Lilly
with her, so that means Lilly is still in the house," his voice carried a
calm confidence.

Then they noticed Mrs. Waters adjust the angle of the car and
she drove it forward instead, right past where they were, towards the
back of the house. The two men watched in silence, unsure of what
to think about her actions. They watched as she drove the car toward
the back field and into the surrounding trees.

"What the fuck?" Frank's mouth fell open in disbelief.

"Frank, walk down the field in that direction and see if you
can tell where she went. I'll stay here and cover the house. Don't let
yourself be seen though, and don't you dare make any moves on her
without letting me know. He pulled a pair of walkie talkies from his
bag, hit the switch, turned down the volume and tossed one at his
partner.

Frank didn't hesitate. He took off in the direction they'd seen
her drive as swiftly and quietly as he possibly could. The field was
fairly long, and the grass stood tall, covering him from sight with

ease. He was nearly in the woods when he heard the snapping of twigs. He halted his steps and crouched down in silence. Mrs. Waters emerged from the woods and walked firm and proud back to the house. He waited for her to be out of earshot before he flipped on the walkie talkie.

"Should I come back, or go find the car? Frank asked.

"Go find the car. I'll keep an eye on her," replied Daniel.

"Copy that."

Daniel watched as the woman walked the length of the yard back up to the front porch. Her arms were crossed over her chest and her face was stony, as if deep in thought. She slowed briefly as she passed the storm cellar, her eyes peered downward, and then she moved forward at the same determined pace. Once she was inside the house, Daniel could do nothing but wait for his partner to give him some kind of idea of what to do next. Mutely, he sat and waited. He noticed lights and shadows moving from within the house, but nothing alarming. Frank was good at checking in every few minutes.

"I'm following the tire trail. Will get back to you," he informed Daniel.

Daniel waited in anticipation. He didn't quite know what to make of any of this.

Within minutes, he heard a huge crash from inside the house. His whole body tensed up. He reached for his walkie talkie and called his partner. Nothing but static responded. He yelled once more into the walkie talkie and this time he heard a gargled response from the other end. Another crash from inside sent him running towards the house. Feeling defeated, he yelled to Frank that he was going in and then he clipped the walkie talkie to his belt and replaced it with his gun.

Hastily, he ran through the front doorway with his gun drawn and ready. The house was dimly lit, but there was no one to be seen. He pointed his gun and peered into the dining room first, but found it clear. He made his way to the room across the hall, flipped on the light switch to get a better look and it, too, was clear. He wasn't sure where to go next, and then he heard a rumble from the floor below him. Quickening his pace, he tried to find a way downstairs.

He approached a living room that was dark with the exception of a gentle glow on the television. There were cartoons on and a little girl sat in front of it. She eyed the detective, but she didn't seem afraid. He approached her cautiously, and he repositioned his gun behind him so he wouldn't frighten her. Kneeling in front of her, he could see she was about three or four years old. She had straight blonde hair that reached halfway down her back.

"What's your name?" he asked, with a cardboard smile plastered on his face.

She had her index finger in her mouth as she chewed on its tip. A soft voice emerged from her throat. She was picking at her lip, making her apprehension of the stranger clear.

"Marie."

"Marie. That is a beautiful name. Where is your mommy?" he asked quickly, but he tried to mask his concern by lowering his voice to a gentle murmur.

The little girl didn't speak for a moment, and then she whispered, "She isn't my mommy," as she pointed in the direction of the back of the stairs. In the same moment, he heard another crashing sound from below him. He didn't have time to sort out the little girl's story.

"Listen, if you go outside, you'll find a man. He's my best friend, and he wants to help you. Press the button on this walkie talkie and say the name Frank," Daniel instructed. He placed the walkie talkie in the little girl's hand and she took it with trembling fingers.

"Now you give it a try," he gently ordered as he placed her fingers over the button. She held the object over her mouth and pressed the button as instructed. Her quiet voice uttered Frank's name. Daniel smiled at her, pleased that she listened so well to him. "Good. Good job!" He helped her stand and pointed toward the front door.

"You go now and find my friend Frank. He'll make you safe, okay?" He waited and watched as the little girl walked robotically toward the front door. Her feet moved slowly, as if she was unsure if she should go or not. He wanted her out of the house and he silently prayed she'd find Frank as promised. He watched her until she made it to the porch. She turned around as she reached the threshold and he motioned her to go further.

Once she was gone, he rushed toward the direction she pointed to moments before. He threw the door open and found the room below was dark. He heard a final thump and then silence. He inched his way down the steps, hoping he wasn't announcing his presence to whoever it was down there. Once he reached the bottom and rounded a corner that revealed a dark room, he spotted a flashlight on the floor facing the wall.

It was enough light to reveal the silhouette of a body on the ground. He couldn't make out any more movement in the room, so he inched forward to grab the flashlight. He aimed the light onto the body on the floor and, to his bewilderment found Dr. Stevens. His heart gave a thud. Daniel could see blood and he feared the worst. He wanted to check on the doctor for signs of life, but he knew he wasn't alone in the room. Someone did this to the doctor.

A chill ran up and down his spine as he realized the vulnerability he just placed himself in. He turned toward the stairs and as soon as his gaze reached that direction; he spotted Mrs. Waters lunging at him from the darkness. He didn't have a chance to brace himself for the impact. He went down hard and his gun flew from his grasp.

Horror washed over him when he saw Mrs. Waters lunging for the gun. He recovered from his fall and dove in her direction, thinking he could just knock her away from the gun. His plan didn't work, however, because it knocked her flat on top of it.

"Shit!" he said.

She was dazed by the fall and was just beginning to shake it off when he threw his body on top of her. She found the gun and wrapped her fingers around it as he yanked her to a standing position. She bit Daniel hard on his hand and sent an elbow blow right into his lungs. He fell backward, jolted breathless by the blow. He tripped over Dr. Stevens' body and fell backwards onto the cold, dirty floor, hitting his head on something hard as he fell. He shook off the pain and turned, looking for the woman who attacked him.

When he turned, he was looking into the barrel of his own gun. He braced himself for his impending doom. Then, somewhere behind Mrs. Waters, he could feel a breeze and a soft glow of a flashlight. Mrs. Waters sensed it too and turned to face the intrusion. Frank was descending blindly into the storm shelter through the outside storm doors.

Daniel froze for a split second. He couldn't let his partner succumb to the taste of a bullet and with the last of his strength he slammed his body into Mrs. Waters, sending her crashing to the ground right under the storm door steps. He grabbed the shovel and smashed it down onto her head. There was a crunching sound as the shovel hit its mark.

Daniel was utterly wasted by the fight with Mrs. Waters. Blood trickled down his lip into his mouth. His breathing came in quick puffs as he fought the urge to fall on the motionless woman. He watched as his partner entered the room with a great sense of surprise and confusion on his face. Frank reached up and pulled on a string, bringing light to the cold dungeon.

He swept his eyes across the room, spotting Dr. Stevens and Mrs. Waters on the floor. Daniel was leaning against a wall, bleeding and panting.

"Damn it! Why do I always miss all the fun?"

Daniel looked at his partner and stifled a laugh. He was pretty damn glad to hear his buddy's sarcasm once again.

Chapter 30

It wasn't long after the bodies were brought to the hospital when the article about Lillian Beth Strouse was found on Dr. Stevens, who was under constant care in the ICU. The search for Lilly Waters was called off abruptly. It felt like a door had unexpectedly slammed in their faces. It came as a shock when they realized Lilly Waters wasn't really a three-year-old girl.

It was explained by psychologists that Beth Waters was suffering from pregnancy induced memory recall. They discovered that Beth was remembering her own kidnapping that occurred when she was three years old. She used the defense mechanism of suppressing the horrible things that happened to her at the hands of Dr. Victoria Owens, who was living under the alias of Jean Victoria Waters, her maiden name. Beth's memories remained suppressed and well-hidden until the hormones due to pregnancy overcame her rational mind, forcing the long-hidden memories to resurface.

The little girl found at the scene was Marie Deslauriers, who'd been reported missing over a year ago, from Oklahoma City. Frank and Daniel insisted on personally delivering Marie to her parents. It was a bittersweet moment. They walked with her down to the waiting area in the hospital emergency wing once they heard the parents had arrived. There was a sense of accomplishment when Daniel released the little girl's hand and she ran and jumped into her mother's arms. She turned around as they were walking out and waved to the detectives. Gratitude glistened in her eyes. As she waved her tiny hand, they were reminded that this time they found the missing child alive. Daniel bit his lip to keep from tearing up, but when he looked at Frank, he saw a stream of tears sliding down his face. Frank wasn't modest about his emotions. Daniel's heart was full. His faith was finally renewed, and it was worth every bit of what they'd been through.

They were uncertain how many children Mrs. Waters had taken through the years. The town of Weshure and the FBI had a lot of ground to uncover at the Waters' estate. Apparently, Mrs. Waters was a mastermind at covering her tracks, and the fact that she was dead left them very few answers. The police felt certain they'd have a tangled case to unravel. Box after box of evidence was being removed from the house every hour. Being a doctor and prided citizen made it easy for her to live a false life. No one ever suspected her little secret, and it took another doctor to finally root her out.

Dr. Stevens was recovering from the brutal beating he suffered at the hands of Mrs. Waters. Daniel was relieved he'd shown up when he did and even more grateful Frank had appeared when he did. Otherwise, he and the good doctor would have just been two lifeless heaps on the cellar floor. Daniel had never in his life been closer to death. He decided in that moment that his life needed to change. For the first time, he wanted to find someone like Frank had to live his life with. He finally felt he could allow himself to live fully. His dark days had come to an end, and his self-doubt and pity seemed suddenly very selfish. He needed to accomplish more than just long hours and solved cases. He needed to live, and he vowed he would.

Beth, on the other hand, was another story.

Daniel had no idea how shattered her mind was. As her hormones began to balance, her memories faded. He felt sorry for her and hoped she'd be able to heal from the past and be a healthy mother for her newborn daughter Lilly, but after seeing her in the psych ward, he wasn't so sure.

She was muttering to herself and talking to people who weren't there. She'd even taken to drawing varied images of Lilly to pass the time. The last glimpse Daniel saw of her, she was sitting on the floor with her legs crossed like a child. Her real parents, who were prepared to see her through, stood by her side as she talked about wanting to go outside to play. She seemed to bounce between realities like a ping-pong ball. Fortunately, before she slipped too deeply into the abyss of insanity, she had one moment of reason.

She requested Lilly be placed in Anna's care while she recovered. Anna, with tears spilling down her face, graciously accepted. She'd finally get to have a little girl to hold once again. The baby couldn't have found a better place to grow while her mother tried to heal. Daniel couldn't help but think about how strangely everything was falling into place. The week had been such a horrific whirlwind and suddenly it was slowing down and falling like lost puzzle pieces finding their rightful place.

The world had been touched by the abduction of Lilly. Daniel himself would forever be changed by this case.

The instincts he prided himself on were challenged. His life was nearly ended by his careless judgment. He stared right into Mrs.

Waters's eyes when she lied to him; he felt comfortable in her home and never thought it would end up a crime scene. He hadn't suspected she was crazy. He decided he'd study psychology a little deeper because when you're dealing with mentally compromised people, you can never predict what's real and what's possibly a figment of their imaginations. Body language and actions could never be trusted. He knew that now. He sat in his wheelchair as he contemplated his life. As part of hospital protocol, he had to get a ride home. He was waiting for Frank to pull the car around so he could finally go home.

He couldn't help but smile when Frank pulled up in front of him with a shit-eating grin spread across his face. Frank thought it was kind of funny that he was the only one without a single bruise to show for what they'd been through. Since he was typically the hard ass on investigations, it was usually he who ended up with a fat lip or ripped pants due to a struggle. He'd always teased Daniel about his "standing around and looking pretty approach to police work".

Frank eased Daniel into the car and reached for the seatbelt. "Now let Uncle Frankie buckle you up."

"Knock it off. Get your hands off me." Daniel smacked Frank's hand away. "I can buckle myself in. Thank you very much."

Frank didn't say anything. He just chuckled. Daniel knew exactly how he was going to slap the grin right off his partner's face. Today was the moment he'd been silently waiting for.

"Hey, just for that, I'm planning on asking your sister out on a date. I just thought you should know." He let the words fly in the same moment his partner slammed his door closed. The look on Frank's face was priceless as he stared at Daniel through the car window.

Frank rounded the car and sat in the driver's seat, and with a smile spread across his face said, "Oh, hell no!" He threw the car into gear and roared out of the parking lot.

"Where are we going?" asked Daniel.

His partner grinned as he drove. "I thought we'd pay a visit to our bald, fat ass pajama clad friend on Huddleston Drive," Frank stated flatly with a mocking grin.

Daniel couldn't help but smile.

Thank you all for reading The Abduction of Lilly Waters. If you

enjoyed the book, please share your thoughts on Amazon by doing

a review. Also, feel free to contact the author at

T.M.Novak221@gmail.com.

You can find T.M. Novak on Facebook at

https://www.facebook.com/T.M.Novaks/

She is also on twitter @NovakMTammy

T.M. Novak has many projects in the works. Titles to look for are:

Butterfly Lake; a YA series, Widow's Watch; a psychological thriller,

The Red Headed Monster; a children's book, and The Big GREEN

Dinosaur.